KU-295-389

ROBERT B. PARKER

BLUE SCREEN

A SUNNY RANDALL MYSTERY

LIBRARIES NI
WITHDRAWN FROM STOCK

NO EXIT PRESS

This edition published 2015

First published in the UK in 2007
by No Exit Press,
an imprint of Oldcastle Books
P.O.Box 394, Harpenden,
Herts, AL5 1XJ

© Robert B. Parker 2007

The moral right of Robert B. Parker to be identified as author of this work has been asserted in accordance with the Copyright, Designs and Patents Act 1988

All rights reserved. No part of this book may be reproduced, stored in or introduced into a retrieval system, or transmitted, in any form or by any means (electronic, mechanical, photocopying, recording or otherwise) without the written permission of the publishers.

Any person who does any unauthorised act in relation to this publication may be liable to criminal prosecution and civil claims for damages.

This is a work of fiction. Names, characters, places, and incidents either are the product of the author's imagination or are used fictitiously, and any resemblance to actual persons, living or dead, businesses, companies, events or locales is entirely coincidental.

A CIP catalogue record for this book is available from the British Library.

ISBN
978-1-84344-439-8 (print)
978-1- 84344-321-6 (epub)
978-1- 84344-322-3 (kindle)
978-1- 84344-323-0 (pdf)

2 4 6 8 10 9 7 5 3 1

Typeset in 10.75pt Minion by Avocet Typeset, Somerton, Somerset
Printed and bound by Clays Ltd, St Ives plc

Joan:

resembling or suggesting a fable;
of an incredible, astonishing nature.

1

Many people in Massachusetts thought Paradise was the best town in the state to own property in. Many people in Paradise felt that Stiles Island, off the tip of Paradise Neck, was the best place in town to own property. And most people on Stiles Island thought that an estate called SeaChase was the ugliest piece of property in the country. A few years back, a bunch of gunmen had blown up the causeway that connected Stiles Island to Paradise Neck, and pillaged the island. Only one of the gunmen got away, but he took most of the cash with him. Some people died, and the whole thing caused a selling panic, which a young man named Buddy Bollen was pleased to exploit. He had a ton of cash from some obscure dot-com deal, which he had escaped with when the dot-coms went belly-up. He bought half a dozen of the island's biggest estates, demolished them, and built a single estate said to be bigger than Luxembourg.

A security guard in a blue blazer stopped me at the gate to SeaChase.

'Sunny Randall,' I said.

He checked his clipboard and nodded.

'May I see some ID please?' he said.

I gave him my driver's license, and my detective's license. He studied them.

'It says Sonya Randall on here,' he said.

'That's my real name. But I hate it. I go by Sunny.'

He looked at me and at my license pictures.

'Well, you're better-looking than your pictures,' he said.

'Thank God for that,' I said.

He looked in at the floor in front of the passenger seat where Rosie was lying on her back with her feet sticking up and her head resting on the transmission hump.

'What's that?' he said.

I was offended, but I was calling on twenty trillion dollars and I tried not to show it.

'That's an English bull terrier,' I said.

'I thought they were bigger than that,' he said.

'Standards are,' I said.

I could hear the haughtiness in my voice and tried to sweeten it.

'Rosie is a miniature bull terrier.'

He nodded as if that explained everything.

'Sit tight,' he said. 'I'll call ahead. Check on the name confusion.'

I waited. From the front gate I couldn't even see the house. On the other side of the gate was a white drive that looked to be made of crushed seashells that wound out of sight behind a big rock outcropping. With the car window down, I could hear the surf somewhere and smell the sea. After a time the security guard came back to the car.

'Okay,' he said. 'Follow the driveway up. Somebody'll meet you at the house.'

'Thanks,' I said.

'Dog'll have to stay in the car,' he said.

'She has no interest in going into the house,' I said.

He nodded again and looked down at Rosie through the window.

'No offense,' he said to her.

Rosie was thinking deeply about other things and paid no attention to him. The guard stepped back to the guard shack, and in a moment the big gates swung open and the guard waved me through. The driveway went up and around a curve and up and around a reverse curve and up and, there, facing a big circular drive, was SeaChase. It looked like pictures I'd seen of Mont-Saint-Michel.

'Good heavens,' I said.

Rosie opened her beady black eyes for a moment and looked at me and closed them again and returned to the long thoughts she surely was thinking. So much for Mont-Saint-Michel.

Another blue blazer was waiting for me under a portcullis. I opened my window.

'Ms. Randall?' he said.

'Yes.'

'ID please.'

I gave him the ID. He studied it and my face. He seemed willing to let the Sonya question slide.

'The dog will have to wait in the car,' he said.

'She prefers to,' I said. 'Where do I park?'

'Right here is fine,' the blazer said. 'And leave the keys if you would.'

'Not if I'm leaving the dog,' I said.

He thought about that.

'Okay,' he said. 'Pull it up there.'

I did, and cracked the windows.

'Bye-bye,' I said to Rosie. 'I'll be back soon.'

Rosie seemed okay with that. I got out and locked the doors.

'Are you carrying a gun?' the blazer said.

'I am,' I said.

I opened my purse and showed him the short .38.

'Great conversation piece,' I said. 'Excellent for picking up guys.'

He smiled politely. 'I'm sure you have no trouble,' he said and took me to the front entrance.

It was a double door, probably ten feet high and ten wide, oak and wrought iron. The blazer rang the bell and one side of the door opened. There was a black man in a blazer.

'Ms. Randall,' my escort said.

The black man nodded.

'Buddy is in the theater,' he said.

I followed him into a two-story entry hall with a stone floor and oak-paneled walls. There were swords and shields and pieces of armor hung decoratively on the walls. A huge staircase wound up to the floors above. At the first-floor landing was a bigger-than-life-sized painting of somebody in a maroon velvet smoking jacket. His tie was untied, and the collar of his shirt was unbuttoned, with the points draped over the lapels. He held an enormous cigar and looked magisterial, except that his face was that of a fleshy boy. His unformed boyishness was apparently so insistent that even the subsidized art couldn't conceal it.

'Mr. Bollen?' I said.

'Yes, ma'am.'

'Wow,' I said.

The black blazer made no comment. He led me around a corner and through some French doors and into a small lobby. There was a popcorn stand and a Coke machine and a counter where you could get Jujubes or Sky Bars. Beyond the lobby was a movie theater with six rows of red leather seats and a full-size screen. In the middle of the second row, not wearing his smoking jacket, eating some popcorn and drinking from a huge paper cup, was Buddy Bollen.

'Sunny Randall, Buddy,' the blazer said.

Bollen looked around.

'Whoa,' Buddy said. 'Whoa ho, not bad for a private dick, Sunny.'

I thought I'd start with demure.

'Nice to meet you, Mr. Bollen,' I said.

'Buddy,' he said. 'Everybody calls me Buddy. Even the fucking centurions call me Buddy. Right, Randy?'

'You bet, Buddy,' the black centurion said.

'Sit down, Sunny. Randy, get her some popcorn, a Coke, whatever she wants.'

'I'll pass,' I said. 'Thanks anyway.'

I went down the aisle and sat beside Buddy. His portrait had clearly idealized him. He was short and pudgy, and smoking a big cigar, which looked silly in his soft, adolescent face.

'You want something stronger, maybe? Jack D? Johnnie Blue?'

'No thanks,' I said. 'Could we talk about why I'm here?'

'Hey, Sunny. All business. Cuter than a ladybug's ass, and all business.'

Demure was getting harder, but I held to it.

'You're very kind,' I said.

'Ready to watch a movie with me?'

He drank from his paper cup.

'Coke,' he said. 'All I drink. Classic Coke. Keeps me sharp.'

He grinned and drank some more, looking at me over the rim of the paper cup like a gleeful ninth-grader. The lights in the theater went down. I hadn't seen Buddy do anything. A long, silent shot of grassland came up on the screen. The wind ruffled the grass gently. We could hear it. No other sound. A small figure appeared in the distance, running toward us through the grass. As the figure came closer we could see that it was a woman. Closer still and we could see that she was amazing-looking. She was very tall and muscular, with perfect features and wonderful thick hair, and an easy, smooth stride as if she could run forever. She wore a leopard-skin bikini and high-laced moccasins, and carried a short stabbing spear like the Zulus used. On she came. We could hear her footfalls now, and the rustle of the tall grass as she ran through it, and the sound of her breathing, easy and deep as she came straight into the camera until she seemed to run into the lens, the tiny muscles moving under her smooth skin, and then she was too close and the image blurred and over the blur came the name ERIN FLINT, and it held as we listened to the sound of her breathing, and faded and the title came up: WOMAN WARRIOR. And that held and then the screen faded to black and all we heard was her heavy breathing and then the movie itself came up with the front credits running over the opening scene. The producer was Buddyboll Entertainment.

It was awful. Something about a female superhero in an unspecified outdoor setting, during an unspecified time past. Erin Flint said her lines as if they were transliterated from a language she did not speak. There was some sort of storyline about Erin rescuing the man of her dreams from a series of evildoers, all of whom appeared to be bare-chested weight lifters. Five minutes into the movie, I was identifying with the evildoers. By the end of it I was nearly suicidal. Buddy watched the movie as if it were *Hamlet.* Leaning slightly forward, breathing through his mouth, grunting and nodding at some of the screen moments, he was like someone rooting for the home team.

When it ended the lights came up as silent and unbidden as they had gone down at the start. Buddy ate some popcorn, still staring in a kind of selfless reverence at the blank screen. Then he turned to me.

'Huh?' he said. 'How about that? You like that, Sunny?'

'The opening sequence was breathtaking,' I said.

'Is she something, or what?'

'She's something,' I said.

Buddy tipped some ice from his big drink cup into his mouth and chewed on it. When he was through, he smiled at me.

'And she's mine,' he said.

'Would that be in the contractual sense or the, ah, main-squeeze sense?'

He laughed a kind of *hee-hee* laugh and rubbed his hands together.

'Delicate,' he said. 'You are fucking delicate, Sunny.'

I smiled modestly. He nodded, rocking slightly in his chair.

'We are, you might say' – he winked at me – 'if you was delicate, that we are an item.'

'Congratulations,' I said. 'To both of you.'

'Oh, hell,' he said. 'I'm no prize.'

He laughed *hee-hee* again.

'But I'm rich!'

'That's one way to judge a prize,' I said.

'It is, isn't it?' he said. 'Goddamn it, that's right. It is.'

I nodded. I felt envious of Rosie sleeping happily on the floor of my car. Buddy looked at his watch.

'Let's grab some lunch,' he said. 'And we can talk.'

Lunch.

2

Lunch was served by a young black woman wearing a waitress costume, in a room that looked like an upscale diner, complete with counter and stools. We sat at the counter. Buddy had two cheeseburgers and some fries. I had some tomato soup.

'Now here's the deal,' he said. 'You know I own a ball club?'

'I do,' I said. 'Connecticut Nutmegs. Finished last in the National League in their first year. Your best player hit .281.'

'You like baseball?'

'Not very much.'

Buddy shrugged. 'Well, you do your homework,' he said.

'The sportswriters say that you don't have a big enough market to make a go of it.'

'Show me a rich sportswriter, someday,' Buddy said. 'I got a National League team halfway between Boston and New York. Lot of people like National League ball, but all they got is the Sox and the Yankees. The Nutmegs are a natural rival for the Mets. Look at a map. They can draw on all of Connecticut and Western Mass and Eastern New York State. Once I make them good, they'll pull in people from Vermont, Rhode Island.'

'You seem to have done some homework, too,' I said.

'I didn't get this rich by being stupid,' he said. 'Nothing generates fan interest like a winning club. And I'll get there.'

He put the end of a french fry into the pool of catsup on his plate and stirred it a little before he bit off the catsup end.

'I told my front-office people to go get me the players we need, whatever it takes.' He pointed at me with the truncated french fry. 'But I need to generate a little interest while we're getting good.'

I nodded. I had been with Buddy Bollen for two and a half hours. My teeth hurt.

'So,' Buddy said. 'Sunny. Here's the deal. You seen Erin Flint; she did all her own stunts in that movie.'

'It looked like she did,' I said.

'She's an athlete,' Buddy said. 'World-class. She was track and field in college, threw the javelin, and basketball and softball. Lettered in all of them.'

'I used to row,' I said.

'Yeah? We're in post now on Erin's new picture, biography of Babe Didrikson.'

He paused long enough for me to gasp with excitement. But I couldn't muster it. I nodded.

'You know who she was?'

'Great female athlete,' I said.

'The female Jim Thorpe. Played baseball, everything. Exhibition games against major leaguers, she was great. Hit home runs – amazing woman.'

'And Erin is playing her?'

'Who better?' Buddy said. 'Her sports achievements, her romance with George Zaharias. It's going to rock.'

'Who plays Zaharias?' I said, just as if I cared.

'Ben,' he said. 'Isn't that great?'

'Ben?'

'Ben Affleck. The chemistry between them. Don't sit too close to the screen. You know?'

'Wasn't Zaharias a professional wrestler?' I said. 'Huge?'

'Ben plays big,' Buddy said.

'Of course,' I said.

'So here's the kicker,' Buddy said. 'You're going to love this. I'm going to sign Erin to play center field for us.'

'Us?'

'The Nutmegs.'

'Erin Flint?'

'She can do it,' Buddy said. 'You should see her. She looks like Willie Mays out there.'

'Willie Mays?' I said.

'Absolutely.'

'You really think she can play in the big leagues?' I said.

'You better believe it, Sunny. I'm announcing the week after the World Series. Give the talk shows a chance to hype it all winter.'

'You think there will be any sort of negative reaction?'

'Hell, it'll be like Jackie Robinson. Of course there will be. That's part of the beauty of it. But I'll be on the side of the angels all the way.'

'You think she'll be in any danger?'

'That's where you come in,' Buddy said.

'I'm supposed to protect her?'

'You're the one, Sunny.'

'How about all the security people here?' I said.

'They're men. Erin wants a woman. You can go places with her where men aren't supposed to go. And Erin's a, ah, whatchmacallit, a feminist.'

'And how did you choose me?' I said.

'I had you checked out. I liked what I learned.'

'Thanks.'

'And part of the job, of course, is to keep Erin in line.'

'Meaning?'

'Meaning she's kind of, ah, headstrong. Sometimes she forgets that she's a public figure now.'

'Does she drink?' I said.

'Not enough to worry about,' Buddy said.

'Drugs?'

'God no. No drugs. No red meat. Her body's a freakin' temple, you know?'

'Sex?'

'Hey, Sunny. She's my girlfriend.'

'I know. But I'm just trying to figure out what I should prevent her from doing.'

'She represents me and Buddyboll, and she's the short-term salvation of the Nutmegs,' Buddy said. 'She can't embarrass me, or the company, or the ball club.'

'And if she starts to, I'll know it when I see it, and stop her before she does.'

'On the money, Sunny.'

Buddy *hee-hee'd* with pleasure at his rhyme.

'You want the job?'

'Sure,' I said.

3

Back in my loft I gave Rosie her supper, poured myself a glass of heart-healthy wine, and called Tony Gault in LA, where it was still only three o'clock.

'Sunny Randall,' he said. 'Good memories.'

'Me too.'

'You ever think about the fact that Sunny rhymes with money, and Randall rhymes with scandal?'

'No,' I said.

'Which is why I'm a big-deal Hollywood agent, and you're a small-town gumshoe. What's *your* best memory?'

'How you couldn't unfasten a bra,' I said.

'Okay,' Tony said, 'sure. But once we got past that ...'

'Not bad,' I said. 'I need a little information.'

'You called the right man,' he said. 'Lay it on me.'

'Erin Flint,' I said.

He laughed.

'*Woman Warrior,*' he said.

'I saw the movie,' I said.

'The full title, not *Woman Warrior: The Final Battle,* or *Woman Warrior: The Return,* or *Woman Warrior: The Ultimate Evil?*'

'Nope, just *Woman Warrior,*' I said.

Rosie gave a nasty, demanding yap. She was in front of me, staring at me with a laserlike accusation. After she ate supper she got two rice crackers for dessert. I had forgotten them.

'What the hell is that?' Tony said. 'You still have that overgrown guinea pig?'

'My Rosie,' I said. 'Wait a minute, I forgot her dessert.'

I went and got two crackers and gave them to her one at a time, adroitly, without losing a finger.

'There,' I said to Tony. 'I gather then that Erin has made several Warrior Woman movies.'

'Yeah, sure, it's a huge television franchise. She does a couple a year.'

'The movie was awful,' I said.

'Yeah, and so is she. But people love her.'

'She's something to look at,' I said.

'Too big and sinewy for me,' Tony said. 'She appeals to guys who like to be spanked.'

'I understand she has a new picture coming, a feature about Babe Didrikson.'

'Yeah, she's been banging the producer, who, now that I think, is from out your way.'

'Buddy Bollen.'

'That's right, by God you are a detective. Anyway, he's spent a fortune, which I gather he can spare, on the movie and will spend another fortune promoting it.'

'That's what I was hoping for when I took up with you,' I said.

'And instead you got ecstasy.'

'Or something,' I said. 'Is there buzz on the movie?'

'Sure,' Tony said. 'It's a given, of course, that Erin Flint is an Olympic-level fucking pain in the ass.'

'Artistic temperaments can be hard,' I said.

'Artistic?' Tony said. '*Artistic* is a joke word out here anyway, and in Erin's case deserves to be. She's got the artistic sensibility of a horseshoe crab. For Christ's sake, she thinks she's important.'

'Of course she does,' I said. 'Everyone tells her she is.'

'But nobody means it,' Tony said.

'You represent her?'

'Hell, no,' Tony said. 'She's in the *life's too short* folder. We represent the director.'

'He happy?' I said.

'No.'

'Is she as good an athlete as they say?'

'I heard she was,' Tony said. 'She does most of her own stunts except the dangerous stuff. She's the franchise, they don't let her do dangerous stuff.'

Rosie came over and glared at me again and did another hideous yap.

'Excuse me,' I said to Tony and put the phone down and spread my hands firmly as if I was making a safe sign, and said, 'That's it!'

Rosie looked at me silently for a moment. Can't blame a girl for trying. Then she turned away and jumped up on the couch, made several circles, and lay down.

'Have you heard anything about her playing baseball?'

'Baseball?'

'Men's major-league baseball,' I said.

'Nope, haven't heard that. But Buddy's got a team, right?'

'Tony, you amaze me,' I said. 'Nothing startles you.'

'I'm a Hollywood agent,' he said. 'And it makes a kind of perverted Hollywood sense. The movie will promote the baseball team, and the team will promote the movie. And she'll be the star of each. Man, talk about synergy.'

'You think it will work?'

'No, of course not. But everyone out here will think it's smart, until it all tanks, and then they'll deride the whole idea.'

'What would make it work?' I said.

'Good movie, good team,' Tony said.

'And both depend on Erin,' I said.

'Tank City,' Tony said. 'What's your interest?'

I told him. As I talked, I heard him laughing softly.

'What?' I said.

'I'm just wondering whether you'll shoot her or not before it's over.'

'She's that bad?' I said.

Tony was quiet for a moment at his end of the line. When he spoke again, the laughter was still in his voice.

'Unlike you and me,' he said, 'you and Erin are not a good match.'

4

Buddy Bollen brought Erin Flint to my loft in South Boston. I watched out my window as the limo pulled up and a black Expedition pulled up behind it. A member of the Blue Blazer Corps got out and opened the door and Buddy got out with Erin Flint. They walked across the walk and into the front door of my building, and shortly thereafter into my loft.

Wow.

She was everything she was supposed to be and more. She was actually taller and better-looking in person, with great hair and perfect skin. She towered over Buddy Bollen. And, sadly, me. Rosie got off my bed and came trotting down to see who was there.

'Hi,' I said to Erin, 'I'm Sunny Randall.'

'You'll have to put that dog somewhere,' Erin said. 'I don't like dogs.'

'Her name is Rosie,' I said. 'She lives here.'

'I don't give a fuck,' Erin said, 'if her name is Oprah Winfrey, I don't want her around me.'

'Then go outside and sit in the car,' I said.

Erin stared at me as if I had spoken Algonquin. Then she stared at Buddy. Then she looked at me again.

'Do you know who I am?' she said.

I wasn't sure I had ever heard that actually spoken aloud before. Rosie apparently sensed the absence of simpatico and went back to my bed and jumped up and began to scratch up a nice lie-down spot on my bed.

'Well, do you?' Erin said.

'I do know who you are,' I said. 'Thanks for asking.'

'Well, are you going to put the dog someplace?' Erin said.

'No.'

'Erin,' Buddy said.

'Fuck you,' she said to me. 'I'm out of here.'

Buddy stood in the doorway. He looked like a dumpling blocking her way.

'I want you to stay here, Erin,' Buddy said.

'Get out of my way,' Erin said.

On the bed, Rosie was lying with her head on her front paws, watching us beadily with her black, oval eyes.

'Shut up,' Buddy said. 'You're staying.'

Erin seemed to stiffen. She didn't look at me.

'Sit down,' Buddy said, and pointed to one of the chairs at my table by the window.

Erin seemed frozen.

'Now,' Buddy said.

Erin turned suddenly and walked quickly to the chair and sat down. Buddy gestured me toward another chair with a gentlemanly sweep of his arm.

'No,' I said. 'You take that one. I'll sit here.'

He smiled at me.

'Establishing your turf early, Sunny?'

'I like to sit here,' I said.

Buddy sat across from Erin. Erin was rigid in her chair. Staring at nothing. I sat on a stool and rested my elbows on the kitchen counter.

'Erin's an artist,' Buddy said. 'She has an artistic temperament. It's part of what makes her Erin, but it needs to be guided.'

Rosie apparently sensed that the action was over and the rest would be blah, blah. She still lay on the bed with her nose pointed toward us and her chin on her paws. But her eyes were closed. I envied her.

'I don't like dogs,' Erin said.

'I explained the plan to you, Sunny,' Buddy said. 'And we agreed that Erin needed somebody to help her concentrate on what she needs to do.'

'And that person has to be a woman.'

'Men are good for fucking,' Erin said. 'And not much else.'

'Some men,' I said.

Erin's face brightened stiffly.

'Yeah, lot of them aren't good for anything,' she said.

I smiled at Buddy. He didn't appear offended.

'So I hope you folks can work together. My people tell me you're the best woman I can get to do this work.'

'Good help is hard to find,' I said.

'So talk to each other,' Buddy said. 'I want this to work.'

'Okay,' I said. 'First things first. If you get me, you get Rosie. You don't have to love her. But you have to be nice to her.'

'I don't like dogs,' Erin said.

She had not looked at me since Buddy had intervened.

'I don't care,' I said. 'It's a package. Rosie and me, or nothing.'

Erin didn't speak.

'That's fine,' Buddy said. 'We can live with that.'

'Good,' I said. 'And I'll need some reassurance that in matters of security, my judgment prevails.'

'I don't want her telling me what to do,' Erin said to Buddy.

'I will try to do what's in your best interest,' I said to Erin. 'And, if I take the job, I do not wish to be fighting with you every day.'

'Of course,' Buddy said. 'That's fair.'

'Do you have any questions?' I said to Erin.

She finally looked at me again.

'Are you married?'

'Not at present,' I said.

'Got a boyfriend?'

'Not at present,' I said.

'You live alone?'

'With Rosie,' I said.

'You straight?' she said.

'Yes.'

She nodded as if all that was crucial.

'You don't look very tough to me,' she said.

'It depends on your definition,' I said. 'If you mean can I swap punches with a two-hundred-pound man who knows how to fight? No. If you mean could I shoot him if needed? You bet.'

'You have a gun?'

'Yes.'

She was silent.

After a time, she said, 'You ever shoot anybody?'

'Yes.'

Again she was silent. During the silent periods she would look away. She made eye contact when she spoke.

'You date much?' she said.

'Sufficient to my needs,' I said.

'Do you have sex?'

I smiled and didn't answer. I understood that Erin thought she was supposed to ask questions and she was asking the only ones she could think of.

'You have been married, though?'

'Yes.'

'Divorced?'

'Yes.'

'They're bastards, aren't they?'

'Richie wasn't a bastard,' I said.

'So how come he dumped you?'

'Nobody dumped anybody,' I said. 'We just couldn't make it work and we finally gave up.'

Buddy was fidgeting in his chair.

'So, Sunny,' he said. 'You ready to start?'

'I can't wait,' I said.

5

Erin lived with Buddy Bollen at SeaChase, and while she was there she was protected by Buddy's security people. When she left I went with her, and some of her staff joined us. It took a considerable staff to help her be Erin Flint. She had a personal assistant, a personal trainer, a personal nutritionist, a chef, a publicist, a hairdresser, a makeup artist, a nurse/EMT ... and me. Everyone but me occupied a wing of SeaChase, next to the gym. Every day she went to Taft University and worked in the indoor cage with a hitting instructor Buddy had requisitioned from the Connecticut Nutmegs.

Today, like most days, I sat in the stands near an indoor batting cage and watched Erin work with the hitting instructor. Erin's personal assistant, Misty Tyler, was on one side of me. And her personal trainer, a woman named Robbie, sat on the other side of me. A kid who had pitched for Taft the previous season was pitching to her, and a lean, bald guy with big hands was standing outside the wire batting cage, watching. His name was Roy Linden.

'Don't pull off the inside pitch,' he said.

Erin wore a tight-fitting black tank top and white short shorts and some sort of spiked baseball shoes. She had on gloves and a blue bandana folded and tied around her head as a sweatband.

'Well, what the fuck am I supposed to do?' Erin said. 'Tell him not to throw it inside, Roy.'

'Remember what I told you about clearing your hips,' Roy said.

'So how do I do that without bailing out?'

'Don't clear with your feet,' he said. 'Look.'

He stood outside the batting cage with a bat and showed her.

'If you can't turn on it without bailing,' Roy said, 'don't swing at it.'

'You want me to strike out?'

'If you're doing it right,' he said, 'a ball you have to pull off of will either be a ball, or a pitch you can't hit anyway.'

'Well, tell him to throw me something I can hit,' she said.

'Buzz,' Roy said to the college kid. 'On the plate but keep coming inside.'

When the next pitch came, Erin took a big step and hit the ball very hard into the netting just to my left.

'There,' Erin said. 'See?'

''Bout forty feet foul,' Roy said.

Erin was gazing respectfully at the way the netting still trembled from the force of her hit. Roy looked out at the kid pitching and pointed to the outside of the plate. The kid nodded. He threw the ball again and Erin took another big step and another big swing and missed.

'That was outside,' she said to Roy.

He nodded.

'Waist-high,' he said.

'You told him to throw inside.'

'If you weren't pulling off, you could have hit that thing out,' he said.

'You said it was going to be inside.'

Roy smiled faintly.

'Buzz,' he said to the kid pitching. 'Groove one for her.'

The kid pitched and Erin hit the ball so hard I could hear it sort of hiss as it rocketed over the pitcher's head and slammed into the netting.

'Nice,' Roy said. 'Good one to end on. Call it a day, Erin.'

He looked at we three women in the stands.

'Ladies,' he said.

Then he turned and walked away down the length of the big indoor cage and pushed through the netting and disappeared toward the men's locker room.

I walked with Erin and Misty and Robbie to the women's locker room. There was a private section for the coaches, which was made available to Erin so she wouldn't have to disrobe in front of mortals. Robbie and Misty sat with me on an empty bench in front of some gray metal lockers while Erin showered. I am in pretty good shape, and I'm sort of proud of my body, but Erin, naked, made me feel like a toad. She was so smooth and muscular and proportional, so graceful and centered and entirely gorgeous, and so proud of herself. No move was uncalculated, no position an accident. I checked her boobs immediately. No signs of alteration.

'Looking at her makes you feel like kind of a turd,' Robbie said. 'Doesn't it?'

'A short one,' I said.

Misty nodded sadly. Both of them were attractive in the same sort of routine way I maybe was. Not fat, not skinny, even features, in pretty good shape. Dressed okay. Misty even looked a little like Erin; she was nearly as tall and had the same coloration. But there was enough missing of whatever Erin had so that Misty remained routinely attractive and Erin was, well, Erin.

'She works very hard,' Misty said. 'She works out every day with Robbie. But the truth is, I think she'd look that way even if she didn't.'

Robbie nodded.

'I mean, she looked like that as soon as she passed puberty,' Misty said.

'Really?' I said.

'Yes,' Misty said. 'She looked like that before she ever met a physical trainer. Right, Robbie?'

'She was gangbusters when I met her,' Robbie said.

'Which was?' I said.

'On her first picture, *Woman Warrior*,' Robbie said. 'They hired me to buff her up. Though God knows she didn't need much help.'

'How long have you been with her?' I said to Misty.

'Long time,' Misty said.

'Before *Woman Warrior*?'

Misty nodded.

'Before she was Erin Flint,' Misty said.

'That's not her real name?' I said.

Misty shook her head. 'No. I mean that's her name,' she said. 'I just knew her before she was famous. You know, *Erin Flint*.'

'And she always looked like this?' I said.

Misty grinned.

'From the time she got boobs,' Misty said.

When she was through showering, Erin strolled about naked so we could admire her. Then she put on her bra and slipped her sweater over her head so she wouldn't get makeup on her clothes or muss her hair. I did the same thing. Except I usually got dressed all the way. She stood in front of the mirror over the two sinks, combing her hair and applying makeup. She was still naked from the waist down.

'That bastard,' Erin said as she bent over the sink to apply a bit of makeup to her already perfect face. 'He played with the Chicago Cubs for eight years and hit .268, and he's telling me how to hit.'

'That's not good?' I said.

'Christ, no. You don't follow baseball?'

'Not too much,' I said.

She shook her head carefully so that her hair moved just right.

'And Buddy hired you,' she said.

'It defies explanation,' I said. 'Doesn't it?'

'Where's your dog?' Erin said.

She was still bent archly over the sink like a 1940s pinup girl.

'She's with Richie,' I said.

'Richie who?'

'My ex-husband,' I said. 'He gets her three days a week.'

'You share custody of the fucking dog?' Erin said.

'Rosie loves Richie.'

'Well, it's more than I would do.'

'You've been married?' I said.

'Yes,' Erin said.

'Kids?'

'Oh, God no,' she said.

'How about you and Buddy?' I said.

'Buddy?'

'Yes, do you ever think about marriage?'

'And further contribute to the patriarchy that oppresses us? The hell with that.'

'But you are with him,' I said. 'You're intimate. Doesn't that contribute to the patriarchy?'

'You use what you've got, honey,' Erin said.

She turned from her grooming and stood straight up in front of us, half naked, with her hands spread slightly.

'And I've got this,' she said.

'You use what you've got for what?' I said.

'Buddy's my ticket to ride, honey. And I'm going to ride for all I'm worth.'

I smiled.

'And vice versa,' I said.

'He gets what he wants; I get what I want,' Erin said. 'Where's the harm?'

I smiled as if I agreed.

'Do you really plan to be a big-league baseball player?' I said.

'Absolutely,' Erin said.

She began to dress her bottom half.

'You think you can make it?' I said.

'Absolutely.'

'Have you ever played baseball?'

'Softball. I was a great softball player.'

'But that's a little different, isn't it?'

'I don't appreciate negativity,' she said. 'You better learn that quick if you want to stay around.'

'Just trying to learn,' I said.

Erin effortlessly insinuated herself into a pair of jeans that I would have thought undonnable.

'I can do anything a man can do, and do it better,' she said.

It sounded like something she'd said before. I smiled again in full accord. She put on some lizard-skin cowboy boots and stood and made sure that the jeans were neatly inside the boots. She checked herself in the mirror, liked what she saw, and started for the locker-room door. I went with her. Robbie got ahead to open the door. Misty collected Erin's workout clothes and makeup, put them in a gym bag, and followed. As we walked through the gym and out across the Taft campus, there was no one we encountered, male or female, student or faculty, who didn't stare at Erin Flint.

6

'That's bullshit,' Spike said. Rosie and I were having Sunday brunch with Spike in his restaurant near the rejuvenated waterfront, in the sunny aftermath of the Big Dig.

'You don't think a woman can do anything a man can do?'

'Of course not,' Spike said.

'Is that because you are a bigoted, woman-hating homosexual?' I said.

'Yes,' Spike said, 'but my bigotry is selective. I like you, for instance.'

'Well, of course you do,' I said. 'But you don't think I'm your equal physically?'

'If we had a fistfight,' Spike said, 'I'd win.'

'That's true of most people,' I said. 'Male or female.'

'True,' Spike said.

Spike was a bear in all senses. He was bearded, and massively shapeless, and strong and ferocious and very loving when he cared to be.

'The equality thing gets a little tricky,' I said. 'We're not all equally smart, or equally gifted, or equally attractive, or ...'

I spread my hands.

'I try not to think about it,' Spike said.

He took a breadstick from the basket in the middle of the table and gave it to Rosie.

'She's not supposed to eat between meals,' I said.

'Good thing,' Spike said. 'Don't want her getting fat.'

The breadstick was long and crunchy, and Rosie treated it like a bone. She ate it very effectively and carefully licked up the crumbs from the tabletop when she was done.

'It's a little hard to see exactly how any of us are in fact equal,' I said.

'Inequality is easier to spot,' Spike said.

He gestured for the waitress to pour us more coffee. I knew he was bored with the subject. Spike didn't spend much time in the sphere of abstraction.

'Whatever it is,' I said, 'it's probably best to base it on individual performance.'

'Probably is,' Spike said.

'Buddy is using her,' I said.

Two young men in expensive leisure wear came in and went to the bar. We both watched them. Then we looked at each other and grinned.

'And Erin's using Buddy,' Spike said. 'Synergy.'

'I wonder if he thinks she really can be a big-league player,' I said.

'If she can play, so much the better. Either way, he juices his investment in her movie and the ball club.'

'I wonder if she really thinks she can play.'

Spike grinned.

'If she can play, so much the better,' Spike said. 'Either way, she juices her investment in her career.'

'Do you think there will be a lot of opposition to her being on the team?'

'Like when Jackie Robinson broke in?' Spike said.

I nodded. Spike thought about it and shook his head.

'People will know,' he said.

'Know what?'

'Know it's a stunt,' he said. 'They're used to stuff like that.'

'What if she were actually good enough?' I said.
Spike gave Rosie another breadstick.
'That would be trouble,' he said.

7

I had been out for a run late in the slow Sunday and was still in my sweats, feeding Rosie, when the phone rang. I put Rosie's food down and answered the phone.

Buddy Bollen's voice said, 'Get out here now. Right now.'

Then he hung up. I stood holding the phone for a time, watching Rosie eat her supper. I looked across the living room at myself in the hall mirror. Not good enough. There were only a few people in the world – Spike, my ex-husband, my father – for whom *right now* meant going out looking like an unmade bed. For Buddy Bollen, *right now* would have to mean after I'd showered and changed.

When I looked like I ought to, I kissed Rosie on the nose, and turned on the TV for her, and left her on the bed. I got in my car and drove north through the Ted Williams Tunnel and was in Paradise about an hour after Buddy had called. There was a Paradise police car parked at the Stiles Island end of the causeway, and three more, plus a fire department rescue truck, parked helter-skelter on the oyster-shell tarmac in the big, circular driveway in front of SeaChase. A uniformed Paradise cop stood next to one of the blue-blazer security guys at the front door. He stopped me.

'She's okay,' the security guy said. 'Buddy called her. He wants her here. I'll take her.'

The Paradise cop nodded me in. I followed the security guy down the big front hall. We turned left under the stairs and walked down a long glassed-in atrium passage to the guest complex next to the gym where Erin's entourage was housed. The gym was full of activity. Erin was there, and Buddy, and Randy the black security guy, and most of Erin's entourage, and several Paradise cops, including the chief, who was wearing a baseball jacket and jeans. A guy in a suit with a medical bag knelt beside someone lying on the floor. Erin rushed over to me when she saw me.

'Sunny,' she said. 'They've killed Misty.'

The police chief glanced over.

He said, 'Who would they be, Miss Flint?'

'How the fuck do I know?' she said. 'It's just a figure of speech.'

The chief walked over. He reminded me of Richie. Same strong, medium size, same exact integrated no-wasted motion kinesis. Same capable-looking hands. Same interiority.

'And you are?' he said to me.

'Sunny Randall. I'm a private detective.'

The chief smiled.

'I'm Jesse Stone,' he said.

'How'd she die?' I said.

'Doc thinks someone broke her neck,' Jesse said.

'Medical examiner?' I said.

'We're not big enough to have an ME,' the chief said. 'Doc's a pediatrician in town, but he, like, minored in forensics and helps us out until we can get the county ME out here.'

Erin stood, listening.

'I want you on this case,' she said.

She raised her voice.

'Buddy, I want Sunny on this fucking case.'

'Absolutely,' Buddy said. 'Absolutely, babe.'

I looked at the chief. He nodded in a friendly way.

'Take a look?' he said.

'Thanks.'

'You're on this,' Erin said. 'I'm not letting a bunch of local yahoos stomp all over it. I want a woman on this.'

I noticed that one of the local yahoos was a great-looking young woman in a uniform who managed to look well-dressed even with her gun belt on. The chief saw me look.

'That's Molly Crane,' he said. 'And the large uniform with the rosy cheeks is Suitcase Simpson.'

'Suitcase Simpson?' I said. 'Wasn't there some kind of ballplayer?'

'Very good,' the chief said.

'My father is a fan,' I said. 'I tried to like it.'

'My guy's name is Luther,' the chief said. 'He's grateful for the nickname.'

The doctor had finished with Misty and was now standing and talking with Molly Crane. We stood and looked down at Misty. She was wearing an iridescent blue-and-yellow leotard outfit and seemed fine except that her head was turned oddly. I hadn't seen all that many bodies. But the ones I'd seen always reminded me that dead didn't look like asleep. It looked like dead.

'You don't think it was an accident?' I said. 'Working out, fell, broke her neck?'

The chief took a flashlight from his belt and shone it on Misty's face. I wondered if this was a test. I squatted down beside the body and looked closely at her face. There was a hint of bruising on the cheeks, both sides.

'Someone took her head,' Jesse said, 'both hands, and snapped her neck.'

'Person would have to know how to do that,' I said.

'Yes,' the chief said.

He called to the doctor talking with Molly Crane.

'Time of death, Doc?'

'Last few hours,' the doctor said. 'ME's autopsy will pin it down for you.'

The chief nodded.

'Do you have a theory of the crime?' I said.

'We don't,' he said. 'Miss Flint contends that "they" were trying to kill her and made a mistake.'

'Miss Flint tends to experience everything as being about her,' I said. 'May I come by tomorrow morning and talk with you?'

'I'll make coffee,' the chief said.

'Okay,' I said. 'Now I'll see what I can learn from my client.'

'That would be good,' the chief said.

8

The room shouted *den!* at the top of its lungs. The walls were oak-paneled; the armchairs and sofa were dark leather. There were leather-bound books in color-coordinated rows on the shelves along one wall. There was a fire in the huge stone fireplace. Buddy had assumed a Napoleonic position, with his arms folded, by the fireplace. Erin strode back and forth across the room. I sat in one of the too-big leather chairs and was quiet.

'They were after me,' Erin said.

The striding looked as if she'd practiced it. 'The bastards were after me and they got Misty by mistake.'

'Maybe they were after Misty,' I said.

Erin strode past me without even looking.

'They don't want me to humiliate them,' she said.

She reached the French doors that led to a patio, and turned and headed back across the room.

'They're afraid,' she said. 'They'll do anything to stop me.'

'They can't stop you, Erin,' Buddy said.

Erin stopped striding in front of where I was sitting and turned and looked at me.

'They won't,' Erin said. 'But we'll stop them. I want you on this, Sunny. Twenty-four-seven.'

They both sounded like something recycled from a television movie.

'You want me to investigate the murder?' I said.

'Absolutely. I'm not leaving it in the hands of some small-town cow-shit sheriff.'

'If I investigate the murder, I can't be your bodyguard.'

'Doesn't matter. I'm putting you in charge of the investigation.'

'If somebody is trying to kill you,' I said, 'won't you need more protection, not less?'

'Buddy's goons can do that,' Erin said. 'It's all they're good for.'

'It's all they need to be good for,' I said.

'You told me to hire Sunny,' Buddy said, 'because you couldn't stand having a bunch of macho jerks running your life.'

'Well,' Erin said. 'Things are different.'

'Because you need me investigating?' I said.

'A good offense is the best defense,' she said. 'I want these people caught and I don't want to depend on the sheriff of Mayberry to catch them.'

I nodded. Erin was striding again.

'I don't want to depend on any man to catch them. How hard is a man going to try? Fucking old boys' network. They're all the same.'

'What can you tell me about Misty?' I said.

'She's my personal assistant. Been with me since *Woman Warrior.* She was a PA on the picture and I hired her when it was over.'

That grated a little. I thought back. Misty had said she knew her long before she was Erin Flint in big letters. One person's long time was maybe different than another's, and it was never in my best interest to tell everyone everything I knew or surmised. I filed it for later.

'How about her private life?' I said.

Erin changed direction and began to slowly circle the room. It was a big room, and unless I kept twisting around, I lost sight of her half the time. I decided not to twist.

'She took care of everything,' Erin said from behind me. 'Appointments, meetings, interviews. She handled all my calls, plane reservations, restaurants.'

Erin strode into view again.

'What did she do in her free time?' I said.

Erin paused and looked at me blankly. I smiled. She looked. I waited.

'I don't know,' Erin said finally. 'How the hell would I know?'

'Buddy?' I said.

'Me? I don't know anything. She was Erin's. I didn't keep track of her.'

Erin was circling again.

'She live someplace in LA?' I said.

'She lived here,' Erin said.

'Before here.'

'She had an apartment in my house.'

'LA?' I said.

'Beverly Hills.'

'And before that?'

'I have no idea.'

I nodded.

'She have family?' I said.

'I don't fucking know,' Erin said.

She was in view again.

'Stop asking me stupid fucking questions,' she said. 'And get out of here. Find the fucking people who tried to kill me.'

'It may cost a lot.'

'Price is not an object,' Erin said.

I glanced briefly at Buddy.

'Sky's the limit, Sunny,' Buddy said. 'Just keep a record.'

Away I went.

When I started my car, the dashboard clock said 9:03. Rosie had been alone for more than five hours. Erin was probably sincere in her fears that someone tried to kill her and got Misty instead. And she may even have thought that it happened because she was going to play baseball. She might have felt I would bring something to the investigation, and she might be right. But I was also pretty sure of some other things.

She was coming out with a big movie with a lot of feminist implications. Suggesting she was risking her life to make the movie would be good promotion, and having a bodyguard, and having the bodyguard be female, was probably part of the marketing strategy. Now, maybe she was in actual danger, and I was pretty sure she wanted some big, tough guys looking out for her. Not a 120-pound blonde cutie like me. But she couldn't admit it, probably even to herself. So she asked me to investigate the crime. It would still look good in the press. It was a small-town department. I was a pretty good investigator. And if I blundered onto the truth and brought the killers to justice … how good would that press be?

I wasn't sure she was smart enough to have thought of all this. Maybe Buddy was. Or maybe she was working off some feral Hollywood instinct that didn't have much to do with smart and dumb. I was pretty sure of a couple of things. One, nobody actually knew anything about or gave a goddamn about the late Misty Tyler. And two, I was pretty sure the Paradise police chief was not a yokel.

9

I brought a bag of donuts with me to the Paradise police station. The chief poured us coffee and we each took a donut.

'Cinnamon,' the chief said.

He seemed happy.

'You learn anything from your client?' he said.

'No.'

He broke off a piece of donut and ate it and carefully brushed the cinnamon sugar from his lips. He had on a uniform shirt this morning, jeans, and running shoes. The shirt was ironed. So were the jeans.

'Erin has engaged me to investigate this murder,' I said.

The chief nodded.

'Do you mind?' I said.

'No.'

'Would you like to know anything about me?' I said.

'Your father was a Boston police captain. You were on the job for a while and then went into business for yourself. You're smart. And you don't seem to be scared of much.'

'Who'd you talk with?' I said.

'State police homicide commander.'

'Captain Healy,' I said.

The chief nodded.

'And you're willing to work with me?'

'Sure.'

'Have you had much homicide experience, Chief?'

'Yes.'

'In a town like this?'

'I used to work in Los Angeles. South Central for a while, and then Robbery Homicide, downtown.'

I smiled.

'Well,' I said. 'I guess we know everything we need to about each other.'

He smiled. He wasn't wearing a wedding ring.

'Have you learned anything about Buddy Bollen's security people?' I said.

'Not much,' the chief said. 'Big agency in Los Angeles. Dignitary Protection. They're all bonded.'

'Which doesn't mean one of them couldn't have killed her.'

The chief didn't say anything.

'Fingerprints?' I said.

'Kind of soon,' he said. 'So far she hasn't shown up in the system.'

'Anything surface talking to the rest of the staff?' I said.

'No.'

'Nobody has a record?' I said.

'Nope.'

'Nobody caught in a lie?' I said.

'Nope.'

I might have caught Erin in a lie, but I wasn't sure yet, and she was my client, and I thought I'd sit on that for a while.

'You know her movements prior to the crime?' I said.

'Far as anyone can tell us she was in her rooms at the mansion, and then apparently went to the gym to work out. Apparently, she worked out every afternoon about four o'clock.'

'Who found her?' I said.

'Head security guy,' the chief said. 'Randy Wilkins. He went in to lift some weights.'

'Alibis?' I said.

'Not really. Buddy and Erin were with each other, they say. Everyone else was alone.'

'Buddy and Erin could have done it together and been each other's alibi,' I said.

Jesse nodded.

'Too soon, I suppose, for a motive to surface,' I said.

'None has,' Jesse said.

We ate our donuts and drank our coffee for a little while. There were no pictures of women or children in the office. On top of a file cabinet, near the coffeemaker, was a baseball glove that didn't look new. On his desk was a short-barreled .38 in a clip on a holster. His chief's badge was beside it.

'Erin feels that it is an antifeminist conspiracy to prevent her from playing baseball,' I said. 'She thinks Misty was mistaken for her.'

'I know,' Jesse said. 'Bollen tells me she's going to play for the Nutmegs next year.'

'That appears to be the plan.'

Jesse nodded.

'You think there's anything to the conspiracy theory?'

'I don't care if she plays baseball,' Jesse said. 'Hard to say about everyone else.'

'I don't know what you got from the people at SeaChase, Chief, but all I got from Erin and Buddy was that they knew nothing at all about Misty Tyler.'

'Real name was Melissa,' the chief said. 'Had a California driver's license. Santa Monica address … and don't call me *Chief*.'

'Jesse?' I said.

He nodded.

'Sunny?' he said.

I nodded.

'New best friends,' I said.

10

My father and I had breakfast together every Tuesday morning at the same table, in the bay window that looked out onto Newbury Street. At breakfast time it was my father's table. I was having a toasted English muffin. My father was having hash and eggs. He didn't worry much about nutrition. In fact, he didn't, as far as I could tell, worry much about anything. Phil Randall was the calmest human being I had ever met. It was not self-control, it was an abiding calm at the center of his being. He cared about things. He loved his wife and daughters. But he looked at everything that came before him with clear and unflinching repose.

'How's Elizabeth?' I said.

I didn't like my older sister much, and Daddy knew that. But I knew it would please him if I asked.

'She brought home her latest husband candidate,' he said, 'to meet your mother.'

'She brought him home to meet you,' I said. 'You're the one we both answer to.'

My father pushed some hash onto his fork with a piece of toast.

'I've met a number since she got divorced,' he said.

'What did Mother say?'

My father chewed his forkful of hash thoughtfully and swallowed.

'She warned Elizabeth that he might take advantage of her,' my father said.

'Daddy, she warns both of us that anytime we have a date.'

He smiled.

'Your mother gets a good idea,' he said, 'she likes to hang on to it.'

'So what did you think of the latest Mr. Right?' I said.

'Another Ivy League jerk,' my father said.

'Your fault,' I said. 'You sent her to Mount Holyoke.'

'To major in jerks?' my father said.

'Elizabeth's specialty,' I said. 'Including Hal.'

My father shook his head. 'At least she divorced him,' he said.

'See,' I said. 'Good parenting shows.'

We both smiled. He didn't mention my own divorce. He didn't ask about my love life. He knew that if there was something I wanted him to know, I'd tell him. My father was quiet. He wasn't shy. His quietness didn't make you feel compelled to talk. It was just a sort of bone-deep peacefulness that made me feel safer when I was with him. Richie had been like that.

'I'm on an odd case,' I told him.

He nodded.

'Do you know who Erin Flint is?'

'Some kind of movie star,' he said.

I knew my father never watched anything but ballgames and Western movies.

'Very good,' I said. 'She's also planning to play major-league baseball.'

My father nodded.

'Do you think a woman could play?' I said.

'In the big leagues? Regularly? Not one time as a stunt?'

'Yes.'

'Probably not,' my father said.

'Sexist pig,' I said.

He shrugged.

'That's probably it,' he said.

'Well, I'm now working for her,' I said.

'Erin Flint?'

'Erin Flint.'

'You going to tell me about it?' my father said.

'Yes,' I said.

My father listened completely, as he always did. And ate his breakfast. When I got through, his plate was empty. He sat back and finished his second cup of coffee. A waiter hustled over with a pot. My father nodded. The waiter poured him a fresh cup and topped off mine.

'Police up there mind you being along on this?' he said.

'I don't think they mind.'

'Anybody up there know what they're doing?'

'The police chief seems pretty good,' I said. 'He used to work Robbery Homicide in Los Angeles.'

'Retired?' my father said.

'From LA? No, he's young. He's, like, my age.'

'So what's he doing here?' my father said.

'Change of pace?' I said.

My father shrugged.

'I'll ask Healy,' he said. 'He lives up around there. He may know him.'

I smiled.

'He does,' I said. 'The chief asked Healy about me.'

'Nice to know he's thorough,' my father said.

We drank our coffee.

'Big money,' my father said, 'is access. That would include access to criminals.'

'And Buddy Bollen is big money.'

'That's my understanding,' my father said.

My father was sitting with his back to the window. I could look past him at Newbury Street where well-dressed people walked by briskly on important and obviously upscale missions.

'You think he's connected?'

'No way to know,' my father said. 'But most people with his kind of wheeler-dealer money know what the papers call "underworld figures."'

'Follow the money,' I said.

'People mostly get killed over money, or love,' my father said.

'Or hatred,' I said.

'Back side of love,' my father said.

'I wonder if Misty had a love life?' I said.

'Good-looking woman in her thirties,' my father said.

'And Buddy's got money,' I said.

'See,' my father said. 'You already have a couple of clues.'

11

I talked on the phone with Tony Gault, again.

'Do you know if Erin Flint has an agent?'

'I don't think so,' Tony said. 'I think Buddy Bollen takes full care of her.'

'Manager?'

'Same answer,' Tony said.

'She must have had an agent or a manager at some time.'

'You don't have a prayer in the business without one,' Tony said.

'By which you mean the industry,' I said.

'Exactly.'

'Do you think you could find out who it was?' I said.

'Tony Gault, mega-agent? Sees all, knows all?'

'I assume that means yes.'

'Sure.'

'And put me in touch with them?'

'Natch,' Tony said.

'How about her personal assistant, Misty Tyler?'

'How about her?' Tony said.

'Can you find out anything about her?'

'She ever been part of the industry?' he said.

'By which you mean the business,' I said.

'Exactly,' Tony said.

I smiled three thousand miles away. Tony was Hollywood to his marrow, but he knew it and could at least make it funny.

'As far as I know she has just been Erin Flint's personal assistant,' I said.

'Mega-agents,' Tony said, 'do not find things out about personal assistants.'

'You could ask your personal assistant,' I said.

'Personal assistants to mega-agents,' Tony said, 'same thing.'

'Okay, and anything you can find out for me about Buddy Bollen,' I said, 'I'd appreciate.'

'I can do something with that. He is, after all, a film tycoon,' Tony said.

'Which mega-agents can find things out about,' I said.

'Sure, if the reward is commensurate with the effort,' he said.

'Doing the right thing is not its own reward?' I said.

'For a mega-agent?' Tony said. 'In Los Angeles, California?'

'I withdraw the question. How about Buddy the baseball owner?'

'I know a sports agent,' Tony said. 'He might be useful.'

'If I come out there, could you set me up with some people?'

'Absolutely,' Tony said. 'I'll have my personal assistant call their personal assistants.'

'Whatever happened to secretaries?' I said.

'Secretary is an is an exploitive, sexist concept,' Tony said.

'Oh,' I said. 'Of course.'

'Mega-agents understand sexism,' Tony said.

'I'll bet they do,' I said. 'While I'm out there will you wine and dine me?'

'At the very least,' Tony said.

12

Tony sent a limo to pick me up at LAX. The traffic was backed up on the 405 going north in mid-afternoon, so the driver went off onto Sepulveda and snuck up on it that way. At Santa Monica Boulevard we turned northeast past the Pollo Loco and went on big Santa Monica, past Century City, where Tony's agency was, to Wilshire and east on Wilshire to the Regency Beverly Wilshire. Buddy had said the sky was the limit, and I took him at his word. The Beverly Wilshire was one of my favorite hotels, and it was at the foot of Rodeo Drive, where, surely, my investigation would lead me at least once.

I unpacked and hung up my clothes carefully, leaving space

between the hangers so the clothes wouldn't get wrinkled. I am usually sort of unkempt in hotel rooms. I leave everything out and throw things around. It's not my house, and there are, after all, maids. But this time, I put everything away and lined my makeup in an orderly fashion in the bathroom. If I were to entertain in my room, perhaps this evening, it would be nice and neat.

Then I took a bath. Usually I shower. But today … the tub was so big and the soap looked so lavish, and, facing the possibility of entertaining, a sybaritic bath seemed right. I did my face, combed my hair, put on clean clothes, stashed the worn clothing in a laundry bag, sprayed a little perfume, stood for a minute and looked out my window at the preposterous enticements of Rodeo Drive.

'I'll deal with you before I go home,' I said. Then, squeaky-clean, beautifully dressed, perfectly coiffed, subtly made up, sweet-smelling, elegantly put together, and as neat and orderly as my room, I headed downstairs to the bar.

Tony was at a table with another man. They stood as I approached.

'God, Sunny, you look as good as I remembered.'

He did, too. I hadn't noticed it before, but he looked sort of like Viggo Mortensen. His small, round glasses, which he probably wore for effect, had green rims this trip, and, like a lot of tall, slim guys, his clothes fit him as if he'd just left the tailor.

'I was hoping for better,' I said.

We kissed. He was wearing very subtle cologne. There was nothing intense in the kiss, just a sort of casual Southern Cal kiss, except that Tony gave me a small pat on the butt as we broke.

'This is Boomer Nicholson,' Tony said. 'Boomer, Sunny Randall.'

Boomer was large and fleshy-looking, with a prominent jaw, a big nose, and a shaved head. I had always thought only black guys looked good with shaved heads, and Boomer's head did nothing to change my mind. He had on a tan glen plaid suit that looked expensive but also looked a little tight on him, as if he might recently have gained some weight. With the suit he wore a pale green shirt, unbuttoned, a thick gold chain, a big pinky ring, and some diamond-studded cuff links that probably cost more than my gun and all my ammunition. He sported a lot of chest hair.

We shook hands and sat. Tony and Boomer already had drinks. Tony was nursing a martini. Boomer had something on the rocks, probably bourbon. I ordered a Cosmopolitan. White wine would have been too girlie-girl. Boomer ordered another Jack Daniel's. From across the table, I could almost feel Tony's energy. He had on a black blazer, a white shirt, and a silver silk tie. It was so Tony to dress up at the exact moment that everyone else was dressing down. He was clean-shaven, as if he had recently shaved. Maybe he too had had a long, self-indulgent bath.

'Boomer is the man in sports representation,' Tony said. 'He represents everybody that has ever hit .300 in the big leagues.'

'Almost everybody,' Boomer said.

He had one of those voices that was loud even when he was speaking softly. His whispers probably blared.

'And he owes me a favor,' Tony went on. 'So ask him whatever you want.'

'Tell me what you know about Buddy Bollen,' I said.

'Buddy's a jerk,' Boomer said.

Our drinks arrived. Boomer finished his first one. The waitress took his glass, gave him a fresh one, gave me my Cosmo, and looked at Tony. He shook his head almost imperceptibly, and the waitress went away. Boomer took a pull on his second and smiled.

'It's why God made corn,' he said.

'Buddy's a jerk?' I said.

'You met him?'

'Yes.'

'Then you know I'm speaking God's truth,' Boomer said. 'But he makes it work for him. People see that he's a jerk and they think he's a jerk in all things, you know?'

Boomer took in more Jack Daniel's.

'They underestimate him,' I said.

'Exactly right, Sunny. They underestimate him.'

'How about his baseball team?' I said.

'I represent a coupla his guys,' Boomer said. 'Buddy's a tough negotiator, and all the time with this *hey, hey, I'm just a chubby little frat kid* going on. Like he can't believe I want X dollars for some guy who hit .271 last year.'

'I thought you only represented .300 hitters,' Tony said.

'And a couple guys used to hit .300,' Boomer said. 'They had a .300 hitter on the freaking Nutmegs, and he'd walk more than Barry Bonds.'

'What's that mean?' I said.

'They wouldn't have to pitch to a good hitter,' Tony said. 'Because the rest of the hitters are so bad.'

I wasn't sure I got that, but I didn't want to bog things down.

'Do you know he's planning to have Erin Flint play for him?'

Boomer took another drink. His glass was almost empty. He looked automatically around for the waitress.

'I heard that,' Boomer said.

'What do you think?' I said.

'Several things,' Boomer said. 'Narrow the question for me.'

People probably underestimated Boomer a little.

'Well, do you think she can play?'

Boomer laughed. He caught the waitress's eye and, with his forefinger, made a little circular gesture toward his glass.

'I hear she's really good for a woman,' Tony said.

'Can she play in the major leagues?' I said.

The waitress came with a new Jack Daniel's. Boomer drained the old one and handed her the glass. She looked at us. Tony and I both shook our heads. Boomer took a much smaller sip of this drink.

'No,' he said. 'Of course not. I haven't seen her, but everyone who has tells me she can't hit major-league pitching.'

'Because?'

'I hear she has a long, slow swing,' Boomer said.

'That's a bad thing?'

'Yes.'

'Anything else?'

'Hell, Sunny. I haven't seen her. But she's a woman. No woman has ever hit major-league pitching. For crissake, most men can't do it, either.'

'But men get the chance to try.'

'I don't know how women's lib you might be, Sunny, but the truth of the matter is, no matter how you fucking slice it, the best men beat the best women in nearly all sports endeavors.'

Women's lib?

'I know that,' I said. 'So is it a gimmick?'

'Sure.'

'To bring in fans?'

'To bring in fans, to get media attention, to juice the book value of the team so he can dump it.'

'You think he wants to dump it?'

'Absolutely,' Boomer said.

'And you think he's using Erin Flint to help him dump it?'

'Absolutely.'

'Even if you're right and she's not good enough?' I said.

'Sure,' Boomer said.

He sipped another small sip of Jack Daniel's and put his head back for a moment and admired the way it felt going in.

'By next fall,' he said when he had swallowed, 'they'll have drawn about three million fans. She'll have been on *Regis and Kelly* and *Letterman*. They'll probably both be in *People* magazine and on ESPN, and everybody in America will have heard of the Connecticut Nutmegs.'

'But is it a successful franchise?' I said.

'Of course not,' Boomer said. 'And it never will be. The market's not right, and it won't be.'

'So would a potential buyer not see that?' I said.

'Buddy didn't.'

'So he isn't so smart all the time,' I said.

'He's pretty smart, but he's got an ego. And he realizes now that it got him in trouble, and he's scheming to compensate.'

'And there would be another buyer like him?'

'Sure,' Boomer said.

'Plus,' Tony said, 'he's got a huge movie coming out with Erin Flint as Babe Didrikson.'

'No shit?' Boomer said. 'I didn't know that.'

'True,' Tony said.

Boomer shook his head. 'Synergy,' he said. 'The little bastard.'

'So the baseball thing will promote the movie,' I said.

'You bet,' Tony said.

'And the movie will promote the baseball thing,' I said.

'You bet,' Boomer said.

He took a slightly larger swallow.

'And how do you know all this?' I said.

'A, I'm fucking brilliant,' Boomer said. 'B, the major-league sports world is not that big. Most of us talk to each other. And C, I'm guessing at some of it. But it's an experienced guess, you know?'

'So if that's true,' I said, 'wouldn't the prospective buyer know these things, too?'

'If he did his homework,' Boomer said. 'But they don't always. Some of them don't have a clue. They're rich. They think therefore they're smart. They can do what they want. There's some brilliant guys, own ball clubs. But you won't lose a ton of money underestimating the intelligence of most owners.'

'You sound happy about that,' I said.

Boomer grinned and drank, carefully, some more Jack Daniel's.

'It's how I make my living,' he said.

13

When Boomer left, showing no sign that he had consumed as much Jack Daniel's as he had, Tony and I ordered a second drink.

'What else have you got for me?' I said.

He grinned at me.

'I was hoping you'd be able to remember.'

'We'll get to that,' I said. 'What have you got for me about Erin Flint?'

He took an envelope from his inside pocket.

'Names, phone numbers, addresses: Erin's former agent and former manager. They're both still in business, and would be happy to see you anytime tomorrow. Just call ahead.'

'Thank you,' I said.

I put the envelope in my purse.

'What did you think of what Boomer said?'

Tony smiled at me.

'Boomer knows what he's talking about,' Tony said. 'He comes across as the crude, loudmouthed blow that he is, but he's smart, and people don't always get it. It's why he understands Buddy.'

'Because Boomer's the same way,' I said.
'Yep.'
'So I should believe him?' I said.
'I would.'
'What's the buzz on the movie?'
'*Babe*?'
'Yes.'
'Good buzz,' Tony said. 'They wrote around Erin. And, presumably, will cut around her.'
'Explain,' I said.
'She doesn't have a lot of lines. And she doesn't have a lot of scenes where she needs to show emotion. They'll use a lot of reaction shots of other actors. They'll have her most emotional scenes played without her face showing. You know, turned away weeping, head buried in her husband's shoulders. The close-ups will be Erin looking intrepid … and beautiful.'
'So they think it will work. I heard Ben Affleck was in it.'
'No more. He's out.' Tony smiled. '"Creative differences."'
'Which means?'
'Might be creative differences,' Tony said. 'Might be he couldn't stand Erin for another thirty seconds. Might mean they found somebody better to play the part. Might mean he found a better part in another project.'
'Do they have a replacement?'
'They do. But it is still a totally top-secret matter. Only the most important people in Hollywood know it.'
'Well, aren't you one of them?' I said.
Tony grinned at me and popped one of his martini olives into his mouth. He chewed and swallowed.
'Especially,' Tony said. 'Because he's my client.'
'Not Hal Race?' I said.
Tony continued to grin. He shook his head.
'Well, who?' I said.
He leaned forward elaborately, brushed my hair back from my left ear, put his lips against it, and whispered a name.
'Him?' I said.
Tony leaned back in his chair, beaming.
'Him,' Tony said.

'Opposite Erin Flint?'

Tony nodded.

'They're doing a rewrite on the Zaharias role, of course, to beef it up for him.'

'I can't believe he'd play opposite Erin Flint,' I said.

'Stars are funny,' Tony said. 'There was something in the script he liked. Nice change of pace for him if they revise it.'

'Which they were willing to do.'

'They would have let him play Babe,' Tony said. 'Plus, thanks to his crack representation, there's a huge payoff.'

'You being the crack representation. And he still needs money?'

'His entourage is bigger than several towns I've lived in,' Tony said. 'Not to mention the children and ex-wives.'

'Even so,' I said. 'I can't believe he needs money.'

'He doesn't. None of them do, in your terms or maybe even mine. But they have to live in certain houses and drive certain cars and go certain places and be certain things or they might be thought failures, and the perception of failure in this town *is* failure.'

'And you live here why?' I said.

'It's where the business is.'

'And you're in the business why?'

'You go with your strength,' Tony said.

'And yours is?'

He smiled and ate the other olive from his martini.

'Bottomless insincerity,' he said.

We laughed. I finished my second Cosmopolitan. Tony looked at me quietly. His martini was gone. I didn't say anything. The waitress came to the table.

'Another round?'

Tony looked at me. I shook my head. He gave his credit card to the waitress.

'Just the check, please,' Tony said.

The waitress went away. The bar, which had been nearly empty when we arrived, was nearly full now. There were some understated bar sounds now. Conversation, ice clinking. No hint of inelegance. I looked at Tony. He looked pleasantly back at me. The waitress returned and left the check. Tony took it from its folder, added a tip, and signed it. He put the credit card in his shirt pocket. Then he sat quietly with his hands folded on the tabletop.

Here we are.

I wondered why I was being so coy. I had decided long ago that barring something unpleasant, we would go to my room and have sex. Did I wish to appear reticent, when in fact I was eager? Was it protective or merely a silly hangover, my mother whispering in my ear. *Be careful… don't let them take advantage…* I smiled at Tony.

'Let's go upstairs,' I said.

'What a very good idea,' he said.

14

We lay on top of the covers, propped with pillows, naked in the warm California night, with the air-conditioning on low. We were both tired, and very postcoital.

'You're pretty good at this,' Tony said to me.

'No need to grade each other,' I said.

'True,' Tony said. 'But good is good.'

'My ex-husband used to say the worst sex he ever had was great.'

'A valid point,' Tony said. 'How is the ex?'

'Married,' I said.

'Whoops,' Tony said.

'Big whoops.'

'Well, it does clarify your relationship,' Tony said. 'Would you like to get married again?'

'I don't know,' I said. 'I try to just take things as they come.'

'Clever phrase,' Tony said. 'Given the moment.'

I smiled.

'I don't think about getting married,' I said, 'or not getting married.'

'Do you wish to marry me?' Tony said.

'No.'

'Nor I you,' Tony said. 'Makes things simple.'

'Yes.'

'We don't have to worry if we love each other or can trust each other. That kind of thing.'

'We don't love each other,' I said. 'And I sure as hell don't trust you.'

'No. But we can have a nice time together every couple of years.'

'We're deeply in like,' I said.

'Anybody else in your life?' Tony said.

'Men?'

'Yes.'

'Not really,' I said.

'Any prospects?'

'I don't think that way,' I said. 'I just try to take it as it comes … so to speak.'

We lay quietly for a time, our shoulders and hips touching.

'Do you care if I spend the night?' Tony said after a time.

'Yes,' I said.

Tony turned his head to look at me. I thought there was a hint of dismay in his look.

'You do?'

'Yes. I don't want you to.'

'You don't?'

'And you don't want to,' I said.

'I know,' he said, 'but a lot of women get hung up on that.'

'So they won't feel like slam, bam, thank you ma'am,' I said. 'I know. But I don't feel that way.'

'You don't mind being slam, bam?' Tony said.

'Not as much as I mind having to sleep in the same bed with somebody I don't know terribly well,' I said. 'And dragging out of bed in the morning looking like shit, and having to share the bathroom and make small talk while I'm trying to get my face on.'

'God bless you, Sunny Randall,' Tony said.

We lay quiet for another moment.

Then Tony said, 'What I'll do is, I'll go home and maybe come by in the morning and have breakfast with you before you go see Erin Flint's former representation.'

'That will be lovely,' I said. 'The breakfasts here are excellent.'

'Everything here is excellent,' Tony said.

I gave him a little bump with my hip where it touched his.

'Before you go,' I said, 'would you, perhaps, like a little something for the road?'

'That sounds good,' Tony said. 'Let's see if I'm up to it.'

We rolled toward each other and put our arms around each other again and kissed again. We pressed against each other. After a moment, I spoke, with my lips brushing his.

'Oh good,' I said softly. 'You are up to it.'

Tony ran his hand gently down the curve of my back.

'A hard man,' Tony murmured, with his mouth against mine, 'is good to find.'

We both giggled about that for a while.

And then we didn't.

15

Erin's former agent had an office on the second floor of a two-story stucco building on Montana Avenue in Santa Monica, a few blocks east of 7th Street. She was a very thin woman in her early fifties, with tightly curled blond hair and rimless glasses. Her skin was pale, with very little makeup. She wore dark purple lipstick. She spoke in little spurts, punctuated with little irrelevant giggles. Her gestures were sharp and angular. She wore black jeans and a black shirt with short sleeves. Her arms were thin. Her fingernails were painted dark purple. Her name was Trixie Wedge.

'When she came to me she had nothing,' Trixie said.

'Except the body,' I said.

Trixie giggled once.

'She had that. But she was nowhere. She hadn't done anything. She didn't know anybody [*giggle*]. She was nowhere.'

'And you helped her,' I said.

'I got her acting lessons. I got her an Alexander trainer.'

'Alexander?'

'Posture and breathing,' Trixie said and giggled. 'I taught her how to dress. I mean, she had expensive clothes and a lot of them. But they were in awful taste, you know [*giggle*]? I got her a new wardrobe, and I made sure she wore it to the right places and was seen by the right people.'

'Pygmalion,' I said.

'Excuse me?'

I shook my head.

'Just someone I knew who had a similar problem. What was she doing when she came to you?'

'Doing?'

'For a living,' I said. 'To pass the time. I gather she was not yet an actress.'

'Oh, no [*giggle*], she surely wasn't.'

'So what was she?' I said.

'I have no idea.'

'She never said?'

Trixie giggled and shook her head.

'She married?'

Giggle and shrug.

'Do you have an address for her?'

'You can get her through the studio or Buddy Bollen's office,' Trixie said.

'No,' I said, 'I mean when she worked for you.'

'I suppose so.'

'Could you find it?'

Giggle.

'Now?' I said.

'You want it now?'

'Yes,' I said.

She giggled again.

'Well, okay, I guess.'

She got up and went out of her office for a while. I sat in the small room with its small, cold fireplace behind the desk. There was a gas log but it wasn't lit. On the walls were head shots of a bunch of actors I didn't know and a couple I sort of did. There were also a couple of posters for television movies. I read the posters carefully and looked at all the pictures, and got up and went to the window and looked down at Montana Avenue for a time, and finally Trixie returned.

'My assistant is on her honeymoon [*giggle*], and the files are in disarray.'

'But you found an address?'
'Yes. She wouldn't be there now.'
I nodded. Trixie handed me a piece of notepaper with an address.
'It's in Santa Monica,' she said. 'Off San Vicente, I think.'
'I'll find it,' I said. 'Anything else you can tell me about her?'
Trixie shrugged and giggled.
'She was a bitch,' Trixie said.
'There's always one,' I said.
Trixie giggled.

16

Erin's former manager had a desk in a little cubicle in a warren of little cubicles occupied by a large management agency on Beverly Boulevard. He was a wispy, middle-aged man with a swell tan and thick, white hair worn longish and brushed straight back. His name was Ash Crawford.
'She needed more managing than I could give her,' he said when I asked him to talk about Erin. 'Wild child.'
'Was she married?' I said.
'Said she was. I never met him.'
'Do you know his name?'
Ash Crawford smiled like a happy uncle.
'"My husband,"' he said. 'That's all she ever called him.'
'Where did she live?'
'Santa Monica, near Seventh Street, I think. I used to meet her sometimes at the bar at Shutters.'
'Do you have an address?' I said.
'Bet I do.'
He turned to the computer on his desk and worked for a moment.
'Here you go,' he said.
The printer started up and a page came out. He handed it to me. It was the same address Trixie had given me. There was a phone number, too. But it was not likely to be useful. I folded the printout and put it in my purse.

'So when did you start managing her?' I said.

'Start of her career. She was still trying to break into the business when she came to me. I got her an agent.'

'Who?'

'Trixie Wedge.'

'She a good one?' I said

'She's as good as you're going to get with no track record' – Crawford smiled – 'and no discernible talent.'

'Why did you take her on?' I said.

'The look. You don't see many people who look like Erin Flint.'

'You felt that would be enough?'

'Yes. We could teach her the rest.'

'Talent?' I said.

He smiled again.

'Film can be edited,' he said.

'So you can, ah, create a performance?'

'Sure,' Crawford said. 'It's not like the stage. In the editing room, you have enough film, you can make anyone better than they are.'

'Erin is better than she was?' I said.

'Uh-huh.'

'Yikes,' I said.

'Fearful to consider, isn't it?'

'What was her big break?' I said.

'Meeting Buddy Bollen,' Crawford said.

'How did that happen?'

'I don't know. I didn't know she'd met him until she fired me. Said Buddy was handling her now. I told her Buddy's a producer. It's like the chicken being handled by the fox.'

'What did she say?'

'She said in this case she was the fox, and see you later.'

'Do you know about her new movie?' I said.

'I heard she was making one about some great female athlete.'

'When I talk to her and Buddy,' I said, 'they talk as if it's done.'

'Hell,' Crawford said, 'I don't know. But people like Erin and Buddy, it has been made. Once the deal is done. The rest is just mechanics.'

'Making the movie?' I said.

'Yes. It's like a new car you haven't driven yet. But you own it. It's there in your driveway.'

'All you have to do is drive it,' I said.

'Uh-huh. For Erin and Buddy, most of the hard work is over. Probably never was hard work for Erin. She just has to walk around and look like Erin. And by now, Buddy has his financing wired. He'll have his distribution deal, he's got a director and a line-producer type, whatever his title is, and a full crew to actually make the movie. Buddy doesn't have to do a lot of hands-on. And Erin – the work is hard. Long hours, lotta retakes, boredom, she does most of her stunts, but it's stuff she can do. She gets the biggest trailer on the set, and everyone calls her Miss Flint, and she's a star.'

I nodded.

'When I was married,' I said, 'we had a contractor working for us at our house once. There was a set of kneepads in among the rest of his tools. I asked him if they were for laying tile. He said no, they were for getting the job.'

'Exactly,' Crawford said. 'You understand the business.'

'Oh hooray,' I said. 'How about her personal assistant, Misty Tyler?'

Crawford shrugged and shook his head.

'Don't know her,' he said. 'I assume it's a her.'

'Do you know any guys named Misty?' I said.

He laughed.

'You never know for sure anymore.'

'Melissa Tyler,' I said.

'Never heard of her. She must have arrived after I got the boot. When I had Erin, she didn't need a personal assistant.' He smiled. 'Except me.'

'What was she doing when she came to you?'

'Doing?'

'You know, work, career, whatever. How did she spend her days?'

'Working out, as far as I know.'

'That's all?'

'All I know about,' he said. 'I think she belonged to Sports Club/LA.'

'Isn't that pricey?'

'It is.'

'And how did she get there from Santa Monica?' I said.

He looked at me blankly.

'Drove, I suppose.'

'So she had a car?'

'Yeah, one of those little Mercedes with the retractable hard top.'

'Not cheap,' I said.

'I suppose not,' Crawford said.

'So what did she do to earn it?' I said.

'Maybe the hubby had some money,' he said.

'She implied a couple,' I said.

'Of husbands?' Crawford said. 'Could be. I don't know anything about it.'

'Was she a feminist when you knew her?' I said.

He smiled.

'When I knew her all she wanted was to be a star,' he said. 'I don't think she ever really thought about anything else.'

'Now she is a feminist.'

'She plays a kind of female Schwarzenegger,' he said.

'So she is living up to the role,' I said.

'Uh-huh,' he said. 'And now she's a star.'

'Stars are feminists?'

'Most of the stars are liberal,' Crawford said. 'Except for the Mel Gibson wing. But the official position for a star is feminist, antiracist, gay rights, antiwar, civil liberties, environmental. Their views aren't righter or wronger than those held by any collection of airheads. Say me, for instance, and you. But stars have access, so what they think actually gets treated as if it mattered.'

'Which it doesn't,' I said.

'No more than your opinion or mine,' he said.

'Nor, I suppose, any less,' I said.

Crawford sat back from his little desk in his little cubicle with his hands folded across his flat stomach. He smiled.

'Maybe a little less,' he said.

17

The address in Santa Monica, which Erin Flint had once used, was a stucco bungalow down 7th Street Hill and bear left in the Canyon. It was surrounded by flowers and had an oblique but discernible view of the ocean. I parked on the street and walked to the front door. There was the California smell: flowers, fruit trees, olives smashed on the sidewalk, the mild astringency of the sea air from the Pacific. It was November. When I had left Boston it was 27 degrees and gray. Santa Monica, this afternoon, was bright sun and 73. The West Coast had its moments.

There was a Big Wheel on the patio, and a barbecue pit among the flowers. I rang the doorbell.

A big blonde woman answered. She was wearing a yellow tank top and white short shorts and no shoes. Her hair was in a long single braid, and she looked like I'd always imagined a Rhine maiden would look.

'Hi,' I said. 'My name is Sunny Randall and I'm a detective from Boston looking into a matter for Erin Flint.'

'The movie star?' the Rhine maiden said. 'We bought this house from her.'

'I know she used to live here,' I said.

'Her and her sister,' the Rhine maiden said. 'Though she wasn't Erin Flint when we bought it from her.'

'Really?' I said. 'Can we talk?'

'Sure, come on in,' she said. 'Want some coffee?'

'Thanks, I'd love some,' I said. 'You are?'

'Oh, I'm sorry, I'm Janey Murphy. Mrs. Charles Trent actually, but I use my birth name.'

Janey Murphy. So much for Rhine maiden. We sat in her kitchen at a freestanding tile-top counter and she poured us coffee. The sound of kitchen activity brought a sleepy-looking bulldog lumbering hopefully in from wherever he'd been recently asleep.

'Ohmigod,' I said, 'a dog. I'm in dog withdrawal. May I pat her?'

'Of course,' Janey said. 'Her name is Sprite.'

The dog lumbered over and sat by my foot. I got off the stool and crouched down to pat her. She wasn't after patting. She was after food. But she accepted patting with dignity. Better, no doubt, than nothing.

'Sprite?' I said. 'What does she weigh?'

'Sixty pounds,' Janey said.

'That's sprightly,' I said.

'My husband has an odd sense of humor,' Janey said. 'But she's very sweet. She's wonderful with my daughter.'

'I have a bull terrier,' I said.

'Like the beer dog?'

'Yes. But a miniature. Rosie.'

'I'll bet she's adorable.'

'Entirely,' I said. 'So what was Erin Flint's name when you bought the house?'

'It's on the closing documents. Her name was Ethel Boverini. I remember because it so doesn't sound like she looks.'

'And her sister?'

'Edith,' Janey said.

I sat back up on the stool and drank some coffee. Sprite went around the freestanding counter and gazed up at Janey. She took a dog biscuit from a ceramic canister and handed it to the dog.

'Edith Boverini?' I said.

'Yes. They owned the house together.'

'Ethel and Edith,' I said.

'Yes. It's funny. We didn't even know their real names until it came time to sign the documents. My husband's a lawyer. He brought it up at the closing. Delayed everything until he could establish for certain that they were the actual owners and could sell us the house unencumbered.'

She smiled and gave Sprite another biscuit.

'You know how lawyers are,' she said.

'I do,' I said. 'What names were they using?'

'Well, Erin, of course, and the sister. I think Erin called her Misty.'

'Misty Tyler?' I said.

'I don't know. I don't know that I ever knew their last names. They just called each other Erin and Misty. Almost like they were practicing.'

So Misty had known Erin a long time. Since they'd been Ethel and Edith Boverini. All her life.

'You have a daughter,' I said.

My father always contended that when you were questioning people it was good sometimes to make it like a chat. I thought he was right. Especially when they weren't a suspect and you were just vamping for information.

'Yes, she's in kindergarten.'

'And your husband's an attorney.'

'Entertainment law.' She smiled. 'In Beverly Hills. I'm his trophy wife.'

'Good for him,' I said.

She smiled.

'Good for us both,' she said.

'Anything else you can tell me about the Boverini sisters?' I said.

She shrugged. 'House was nice and clean when we looked at it and when we moved in. No surprises. Everything worked as advertised.'

'Any mail ever come for them after they moved?'

'No. It was odd, I mean, doesn't that usually happen? We never got a single thing meant for them.'

'No one ever knocked on the door looking for them?'

'Just you,' Janey said.

'May I give Sprite a cookie?' I said.

'Of course,' Janey said. 'It's part of her job. Eating cookies, sleeping, lapping your face, accepting hugs. I'm not sure she likes the hug part so much.'

'Funny,' I said. 'That's the part I like best.'

We both laughed. Just a couple of girls in a clean, quiet house, having coffee and chatting in the bright kitchen. Husband at work. Kid in school. I envied her.

Sort of.

18

The Los Angeles County birth, death, and marriage records are located in the County Clerk's office in Norwalk, down US5 a ways, not too far from Whittier. I spent some time there, and by late afternoon I knew that Ethel Boverini had been born in April of 1970, in El Segundo, and that Edith had been born a year later, in June. The mother was Rosalie Boverini; the father was unknown. Rosalie herself, if it was the same one, was born in 1955. In the marriage records there was no evidence that Rosalie ever married. But there was a record of Ethel Boverini marrying Gerard Basgall in 1988. And in the death records, I found that Rosalie Boverini died in October of 1987. There was no record of Edith Boverini marrying or giving birth. There was no record of Ethel giving birth.

When I got back to my hotel it was early evening. There was a message from Tony Gault saying he was tied up with clients this evening and hoped we could get together tomorrow. I smiled. Poor baby, probably needed time to build up his sperm count. In fact, the prospect of a long shower, a comfortable robe, a glass of wine, and something lovely from room service was more enticing than Tony after a long day in the records office.

God bless good hotels. My room was orderly, my bed turned back. My ice bucket had been filled. I took a shower and put on a big, white terry-cloth robe, which was pleasantly too big for me, so that it wrapped well around me and I had to roll the sleeves up. I poured myself a glass of wine from the minibar and sat in the armchair by the window and looked out across Wilshire Boulevard at Beverly Hills. The television clicker was on my bed table. I decided against it.

The silent statistics of birth, marriage, and death had told me a lot. None of it told me anything about who killed Misty Tyler, aka Edith Boverini. But it told me some things about the life she and her older sister must have led. Erin, aka Ethel, would have been born, apparently out of wedlock, when her mother was about fifteen. The double names were making my head hurt. I decided to think of them as Erin and Misty. I smiled to myself at the quaintness of my phraseology. *Out of wedlock.* Come to think of it, I too, at the moment, was out of wedlock. Erin's mother died at age thirty-two, when Erin would have been seventeen. She was eighteen when she married. There was no indication that she had ever given birth, at least in LA County. So the girls were orphaned at seventeen and sixteen. And Erin was married a year later to Gerard Basgall. I looked up Basgall in the phone book. There were no Basgalls, but it was only for the west side of LA.

I looked at my watch. It was quarter of ten in the east. I picked up the phone and called the police in Paradise, Massachusetts.

'This is Sunny Randall,' I said to the night-desk cop. 'I don't suppose Chief Stone is still there?'

'No, ma'am.'

'And I don't suppose you can give me his home phone number,' I said.

'That information is not available,' he said.

'Then could you do me a favor? It's part of the Misty Tyler case out at SeaChase. Could you call Chief Stone and ask him to call me at this number?'

There was a pause.

'Who did you say this was?'

'Sunny Randall,' I said. 'Chief Stone knows me.'

'Yes, ma'am. I know who you are. I could try calling him, ma'am.'

I gave him my number and thanked him and hung up and sipped my wine.

Life had obviously not been carefree for Erin and Misty. But why did they keep their past a secret? Why was the sisterhood a secret? She had dressed well before she became famous, and lived in a good house and drove a good car. She had some money. Where did she get it? It was pretty certain she didn't inherit it from Rosalie Boverini. Gerard? There was a lot I didn't know, and the more I found out, the more there was for me not to know. But one thing was clear. Erin Flint, superstar, was a big, fat liar.

I finished my wine and was pouring another when the phone rang. Oh good, it was Jesse Stone.

'I hope I didn't get you out of bed,' I said.

'I'm wide awake,' he said.

'Me too,' I said. 'I'm in LA. Here's what I've found out.'

He didn't say anything while I told him what I had learned.

When I got through he said, 'Be nice if you could run down Gerard.'

'My thought exactly,' I said. 'Do you still have any influence out here?'

'I didn't have any when I was there,' he said. 'But there's a captain named Cronjager. Robbery Homicide commander. He fired me for drinking on duty, but he's a good man and a good cop. I'll call him and tell him you're coming in.'

Jesse had just confided in me. Fired for drinking.

'Downtown?' I said. 'Parker Center?'

'Yes,' Jesse said. 'Third floor.'

'You think he might be in the system?'

'Their vital stats don't tell me they were hanging out with polo players.'

'Worth a try,' I said.

'Even if he's not in the system. Cronjager has resources.'

'Okay, I'll go see him tomorrow morning.'

'If there's a hitch,' Jesse said, 'I'll call you. Otherwise, go ahead. He'll be expecting you.'

I gave him my cell-phone number. He gave me his. It was like deciding to go steady.

'Remember one other thing,' Jesse said. 'The police chief out there is a Boston guy.'

'My God, that's right,' I said. 'It was while my father was on the job. My father always said what a wonderful cop he was.'

'That's what they tell me,' Jesse said.

'So if Cronjager doesn't work out …' I said.

'Cronjager's okay,' Jesse said. 'I'll call him.'

I wanted to talk some more. I liked hearing his voice. But I couldn't think of anything else to say. And Jesse seemed to have no interest in chatting. So I said good-bye.

After I hung up I sipped my second drink and thought about how much I liked Jesse on such brief acquaintance. Then I picked up the room-service menu and began to concentrate on what to eat. The menu told me all I needed to know. The clarity was gratifying.

19

Cronjager had a nice office, big, with a window. He stood when I came in and walked around the desk to shake hands with me. He was a tall man, sort of rangy, with an assertive nose and snow-white hair. His skin was tanned and he looked healthy. His handshake was hard but not showy.

'Jesse Stone said you'd be in. Fine officer, Jesse.'

'He told me you fired him for drunkenness.'

Cronjager smiled a little and went back around his desk. He indicated a chair for me and sat down. I sat across from him.

'So much for professional discretion,' he said. 'I understand he's got it under control.'

'Seems to be in remission, at least.'

'Good,' Cronjager said. 'Waste of a very good cop.'

'Did he tell you why I'm here?'

'No. Just said you were smart and good-looking and I'd enjoy you.'

'Wow,' I said.

'So far he's right,' Cronjager said. 'What do you need?'

'Jesse and I are working on the same case,' I said, and told him about it.

'Erin Flint,' he said when I was through. 'Can't act, but something to see.'

'She was married once, under what appears to be her birth name, Ethel Boverini, to a man named Gerard Basgall.'

'And you'd like me to help you find Gerard,' Cronjager said.

There was something about him that was like my father. They didn't look alike, but they had a quality of courtliness. Older tough guys who had seen everything, men for whom time and experience had somehow smoothed the hard edges and made them graceful.

'My father was a captain,' I said.

'Boston?' Cronjager said.

'Yes. Like you, homicide commander.'

'Retired?'

'Yes.'

Cronjager smiled.

'I should be,' he said.

He picked up a phone and said something into it and put it down. In a moment a Hispanic woman came briskly into the room. Her clothes were good. Her gray/white hair was stylish. Cronjager stood when she entered.

'Elaine Estallela,' Cronjager said. 'Sunny Randall.'

We each said, 'How do you do.'

Cronjager said, 'Sunny's looking for somebody named Gerard Basgall, Elaine. Think he might be in the system?'

Elaine smiled.

'That means,' she said to me, '"Elaine, would you look him up because I'm afraid of the computer."'

Cronjager and I both smiled. Elaine walked to a side table and tapped the keys of a computer keyboard. The screen lit up.

'Any cross-references?' Elaine said.

'He's been married…' Cronjager looked at me.

'He married Ethel Boverini,' I said. 'In 1988.'

Standing in front of the screen, Elaine tapped the keyboard some more. She was an attractive woman, and graceful. I wondered if she might be younger than her gray hair suggested.

After a time she said, 'Mr. Basgall is in the system.'

'Whaddya got?' Cronjager said.

Elaine began to read off the screen.

'1986, living off the earnings. 1988, living off the earnings. 1988, assault. 1991, possession with intent. 1994, extortion.'

'Gerard Basgall,' Cronjager said, 'the early years.'

'Anything on Mrs. Basgall?' I said.

'Not so far,' Elaine said. 'Assault. Extortion. Oh, look. Gerard was twice arrested on suspicion of murder – 1997, 1998. Insufficient evidence.'

'Working his way up,' Cronjager said.

'Maybe he made it,' Elaine said. 'After 1998 there's no arrests.'

'Gee,' I said. 'Maybe he went straight.'

'That's probably it,' Cronjager said.

Elaine continued to look at the computer screen.

'Sheriff's Department Career Criminals unit has been interested in him,' she said. 'Since at least 2000.'

'Or maybe he didn't,' I said.
'Who's running that?' Cronjager said.
'Career Criminals?' Elaine said. 'Doreen Billups.'
'Get her for me, would you, Elaine?'
She smiled. 'When I reach her,' Elaine said, 'will you be able to hold the phone all right by yourself?'
'Long as you tell me which end to talk in,' Cronjager said.
Elaine made the call from a phone on the computer table. When it went through, she said, 'Captain Billups? Captain Cronjager is calling,' and pointed at the phone on his desk.
Cronjager picked it up.
'Doreen?' he said. 'Yeah … yeah … How's Harvey? … good, and the kid? … UCLA? … for crissake, Doreen, I thought he was still in junior-high … yeah, I know … she's fine, thanks … listen, I see on this here computer I'm so good with that your people are interested in a fella named Gerard Basgall … yeah, right there on the screen … well sure Elaine helped a little … uh huh … uh huh … sonovabitch, excuse me, Doreen … uh-huh … okay, well Gerard's done all right, hasn't he? … Yeah. Got a detective here from Boston, good-looking woman named Sunny Randall. She needs anything, can she call you? Yes. Elaine'll give her the number … sure, anything you got. Send it to me, I can get it to Sunny … and thank you, Doreen. Yeah, you too.'
Cronjager put the phone back.
'That where it goes?' he said.
Elaine smiled and nodded. He leaned back in his chair.
'Okay,' he said to me. 'Gerard is a big success. He's head pimp in the Valley.'
'Meaning?' I said.
'He runs all the call-girl operations north of Sunset,' Cronjager said, 'between, oh, say, Thousand Oaks and maybe Pasadena.'
'Any mention of Ethel Boverini?' I said.
'No.'
'Have an address for Gerard?'
'I do,' Cronjager said and wrote it out on a piece of notepaper.
'Bel Air,' I said. 'I think I'll go see him.'
'I'll have somebody take you,' Cronjager said.
'I know how to get to Bel Air,' I said.

'I have somebody take you, there's no parking issues,' Cronjager said. 'No hassle.'

'I'll be fine.'

'And you'll have an official presence,' Cronjager said. 'Be easier to get in.'

'And out,' Elaine said.

'See if you can get Sol up here,' Cronjager said.

'You think Gerard is dangerous?' I said.

'I'm just a civilian employee,' Elaine said. 'But pimps don't generally respect women.'

'And keeper of the captain,' Cronjager said.

Elaine nodded that this was so, and picked up the phone.

Cronjager smiled at her, then looked at me and said, 'If you're investigating a murder, Ms. Randall, somebody you talk with might be a murderer.'

'I'll wait for Sol,' I said.

20

We went out Sunset from downtown, west toward Bel Air. My driver, Sol Hernandez, looked like Lieutenant Castillo in *Miami Vice,* which was on television when I was in college. The girls I knew in college thought Lieutenant Castillo was hot. Me too.

'Sol?' I said. 'Hernandez?'

'Short for Solario,' he said.

We passed Chavez Ravine, where the Dodgers played, drove through Silver Lake and on through Hollywood under a high, hot sun. Even in the least savory neighborhoods there were flowers and trees and the smell of vegetation. The out-of-town weather section of the *L.A. Times* this morning showed Boston with snow, accumulating to three inches.

Sigh.

We went along the Strip in West Hollywood. Sol was blessedly quiet. He did not point out landmarks. In Beverly Hills the greenery intensified, and when we turned into the Bel Air gate past Beverly Glen it felt like I was in Tahiti. We wound uphill until we pulled into the big driveway of a vast, white stucco house with a red tile roof.

'Gerard appears to have done well for himself,' I said.

'Head pimp,' Sol said.

We got out and walked to the front door. Sol had his shield folder tucked into the breast pocket of his cream-colored linen jacket so that the shield showed. I rang the bell. Time passed, and I could sense more than I could hear somebody studying us through the peephole. Then the door opened a few inches on a security bar. A man's face appeared in the narrow gap. It was tanned. The man appeared bald.

'Sergeant Hernandez, LAPD,' Sol said. 'We need to talk with Gerard.'

'You got some kind of paper?' the face said.

'Just a chat,' Sol said.

'So you don't have no paper says I got to let you in?' the face said.

'We can go get one,' Sol said, 'and come back in large numbers and yank all your fucking asses out of here and drive you downtown in a wagon.'

The face grunted in what might have been amusement.

'Jeez,' it said, 'I think I wet myself.'

'Tell Mr. Basgall we want to talk about Erin Flint,' I said.

'Who the fuck are you?' the face said.

'Margaret Thatcher,' I said. 'Just tell Gerard what I said.'

The tanned face stared at me for a moment. Then the door closed.

'Margaret Thatcher?' Sol said.

'I figured it had more clout than Sunny Randall,' I said.

'I suppose it can't have less,' Sol said.

In a few minutes the door opened and the guy with the tan stood in it. He was bald and kind of fat, but what my father used to call 'hard fat.' He had on a loose-fitting blue sport shirt with big, red flowers on it. It was not tucked in. I could see that he had a gun under the shirt.

'Follow me,' he said.

The house as we walked through it was huge and full of artifacts, and had the lived-in warmth of a shopping mall in West Covina.

'How charming,' I said to Sol. 'Tasteful yet inviting.'

He smiled without speaking.

Gerard was waiting for us in the atrium. In the cool, glassed-in space we could look west and see the ocean, and south and east, nearly all of the Los Angeles basin. There was no visible smog today, and the vista was in fact breathtaking.

'Wow,' I said.

'Cool, huh?' Gerard said. 'Paid a lot for this view.'

'Lotta whores fucked their brains out for it,' Sol said.

Gerard grinned.

'And were happy to do so,' Gerard said. He looked at Sol.

'You're Hernandez, the local cop,' Gerard said. He looked at me. 'But I'm guessing you ain't really Margaret Thatcher.'

I smiled.

'Just a ploy to get in,' I said. 'My name is Sunny Randall. I'm a detective that Erin hired.'

He was a tall man, tall enough not to look out of place with Erin Flint. And he was well set up, athletic-looking. Tanned, clean-shaven, with dark hair cut very short in a military buzz cut. Two large pictures sat on easels, one in each corner of the atrium. One was of Gerard in some sort of martial-arts outfit, executing some sort of martial-arts move. In the other corner was Erin Flint in her Woman Warrior incarnation, hurdling a lion, wearing few clothes, carrying a short spear, and showing a lot of fabulous skin.

'So what's up with Erin?' Gerard said. 'She okay?'

'A friend of hers was killed, Misty Tyler.'

Gerard nodded.

'Did you know Misty?'

'No.'

It didn't seem likely he could have been married to Erin and not know sister Misty. But that didn't have to mean much. Guys like Gerard routinely lied to the cops unless there was some good reason not to. At the moment, I was the cops, and there wouldn't have seemed to Gerard to be any good reason not to.

'You were married to Erin,' I said.

'Still am,' Gerard said.

'But you're not together.'

He shook his head.

'Broads,' he said. 'Present company excluded, Sunny.'

'Of course,' I said. 'Why did you, ah, part?'

'She dumped me. I set her up, gave her money for clothes, for cars, bought her a house in Santa Monica … she saw the chance to fuck some movie producer and off she went.'

I widened my big, blue eyes innocently.

'She'd leave this house?' I said.

'I didn't have this house when she left.'

'When would that have been?'

'Five, six years ago. I don't know. Time don't mean much to me.'

'Who was the producer?' I said.

'Buddy Bollen. Guy made her into Woman Warrior.'

'And you didn't object?'

'Sure, I objected,' Gerard said. 'But hell, Sunny, there's thousands of women, and just one me. I decided to stick with me.'

'Did you love her?'

'Hell yes, still do.'

'But?'

'But I'm a practical man. Time to move on. I can get my ashes hauled whenever I want to,' Gerard said.

'She work for you?' Sol said.

Gerard looked at Sol blankly for a moment.

Then he said, ''Course she did. I look like a guy runs a shelter for homeless pussy? She worked for me, and so did her sister.'

'Her sister is Misty Tyler?' I said.

'Edith? Yeah. I guess I didn't know her new name. I give them the best outcalls. Clean guys. Movie guys. No whack jobs, nothing kinky. It mighta been how she met Buddy Bollen. I don't remember.'

'You should,' Sol said. 'You were probably more hands-on then. Than now.'

'I'm outta that business now, Sergeant. You should know that. I run an event-management service.'

'You're a pimp,' Sol said. 'You used to be a small-time pimp, and now you are a big-time pimp. But a pimp is a pimp.'

'Don't be bitter, Sergeant,' Gerard said. 'How about you, Sunny? I could make you rich.'

'In event management?'

'Four, maybe five events a week, a few hours, evening work,' Gerard said. 'No heavy lifting.'

I shook my head.

'Enticing offer,' I said. 'But I'll pass. Talk more about Erin and Misty.'

'Love those names,' Gerard said and laughed. 'They wasn't so much when I met them. They were kids. I think Erin was maybe eighteen, dragging her kid sister around. Didn't know how to look, or talk. Didn't know anything.'

'How'd you meet?'

'They hustled me at a club in West Hollywood,' Gerard said.

'Tried to pick you up?'

'Yeah.' He grinned. 'Had I ever done two girls at once? Had I ever done sisters?'

'And?' I said.

'Well, truth is I never had done sisters before. But I seen something in them, especially Erin. I mean, she wasn't much yet, but she already had that bitchin' body, and I seen potential. One thing I know,' Gerard said. 'I know women.'

Sol was standing at the window, watching the bald man with the tan who was standing in the doorway watching Sol. Gerard looked at me as if he could see through my clothes.

He said it again. 'I know women.'

'You know whores,' Sol said.

Gerard grinned at me.

'Same thing,' he said.

'So you decided to, ah, represent them?'

'Yeah.'

'And you married Erin?' I said.

'Wasn't part of the plan, but ...' Gerard spread his hands and shrugged. 'I got her clothes and makeup and hair and took her places and taught her how to order. Got her a trainer. Hell, I even sent her to college. I mean, she was turning into something.'

'And Misty?'

'The little sister? She trailed along. Everywhere Erin went, there was little sister.'

'And, I don't mean to be indelicate, Mr. Basgall, but did you have a relationship with Misty?'

'Relationship?' Gerard said and smiled. 'What kinda relationship did you have in mind?'

'Did you fuck her?'

'Whoa, Sunny, pretty direct.'

'Did you?'

'Sure,' Gerard said, 'I gave her a few pops. But I didn't love her.'

'You loved her sister.'

'Like I said – did, still do.'

We talked some more, but there was nothing else to learn from Gerard.

21

On the drive back downtown, Sol said, 'It might have gone better if I didn't ride Gerard like I did.'

'I don't think it made any difference,' I said.

'I know better. In that kind of situation you don't get anywhere antagonizing the subject.'

'Gerard was going to tell us what he told us and nothing more,' I said.

Sol nodded.

'Probably right,' he said.

'You know him before?' I said.

'I used to work vice,' Sol said. 'I know about Gerard.'

'Tell me,' I said.

'He turned up in the early nineties – I'm sure he was pimping for a long time before he jumped onto our screen – he was running a high-class call-girl operation on the west side. Girls were all well-spoken, good-looking, well-dressed. No shortage of those out here. He'd find the ones that looked right and clean them up and train them and send them out to only the best clients.'

'No shortage of them out here, either,' I said.

Sol nodded.

'Lotta money out here,' Sol said. 'Not many scruples.'

'Nor brains,' I said. 'How did he do business? How did he connect the john with the hooker?'

'Mostly hotel staff. Lot of high rollers in a lot of expensive hotels around the west side,' Sol said. 'He'd have a doorman or a bellman or a bartender on commission, occasionally a concierge. He had a lot of limo drivers on the payroll, too.'

'No cabbies?' I said.

'No. He wasn't interested in johns that took cabs.'

'Nice little synergy,' I said. 'The best clientele would attract the best girls, and the best girls would attract the best clientele.'

'As long as you kept the discipline,' Sol said. 'No blow jobs in cars, no stag shows at bachelor parties, no dirty movies – even if it was quick and easy money. Girl broke the rules, she got beat up and fired.'

'Gerard do the beating up?' I said.

'Sure, early years. Now he has employees.'

'He's got a number of arrests for assault.'

'Gerard's a tough guy,' Sol said. 'But a lot of the assault busts are in the early years when he was just a street pimp protecting his investment. Beat up a few johns who got out of line with the whores. No jail time.'

'So why do you suppose the OC squad is interested in him now?'

'He's spreading out,' Sol said. 'He runs the upscale call-girl business on the west side and in the Valley. He's spreading into Ventura County. He's also, they tell me, trying to expand, maybe spread the whore business, maybe diversify – drugs, gambling. Nobody knows for sure. What they know is he's got a connection now with a guy named del Rio, who sort of runs things around here.'

'Should I talk to this del Rio person?' I said.

'No.'

'No?' I said. 'Just like that?'

'Reason number one,' Sol said. 'You annoy him and I can't protect you; for crissake, Cronjager can't protect you. Reason number two, your vic got her neck snapped. Three thousand miles away. It's not his style. He had to have her killed for some reason it would be neat, one bullet in the brain, and no trace of anyone or anything. Mr. del Rio is a dead end, any way you approach it.'

'Maybe he could tell me a little more about Gerard,' I said.

Sol smiled at me.

'You can't get to see him,' Sol said. 'If you could, he wouldn't tell you anything. If he did, it wouldn't be true. Forget del Rio.'

'Okay,' I said.

'Besides,' Sol said. 'Sooner or later Gerard is going to annoy del Rio. He's too restless, too ambitious. He'll do something he shouldn't have, and he'll be dead.'

'Like that,' I said.

'Like that.'

We were quiet for a while.

'You know what doesn't quite work with Gerard?' I said.

'All that chop chop about how he still loves her,' Sol said.

'Maybe it's true,' I said.

'And maybe it don't rain in Indianapolis,' Sol said. 'In the summertime.'

'So why would he keep saying it?' I said. 'It doesn't fit with the rest of him, you know, *whore* and *woman* are two words for the same thing? I loved her but I banged her sister? That Gerard makes sense. But to admit he still loves a woman who dumped him for another guy?'

'Sympathy?' Sol said.

'From us? He knows better. And even if he didn't, he doesn't care about us.'

Sol nodded.

'I know,' he said.

'And the picture?'

'He coulda put it there before he let us in,' Sol said.

'But why would he?'

'Don't know,' Sol said. 'What I know is that slime-bag motherfucker couldn't love anybody.'

I looked at Sol.

'Is there something personal?' I said.

'Yes.'

'Is it my business?' I said.

'No.'

I smiled and shook my head. We were nearly downtown now.

'So many things aren't,' I said.

22

Richie had dropped Rosie off with Spike that afternoon, and she and Spike were in my loft in South Boston when I came home. They both kissed me. Spike settled for one, affectionate and passionless. Rosie inflicted the death of a thousand laps. Spike opened a bottle of Riesling and we sat at my little window alcove and sipped wine together. I had an extra-wide custom chair that I sat in to eat, which allowed Rosie to sit beside me. She sat there now, thrilled to have me home, and hopeful, probably, that we might have something to eat with the wine.

'Eat on the plane?' Spike said.

'Something unutterable,' I said, 'which contained pasta.'

'Best not to think of it,' Spike said.

'Have you been here long?' I said.

'Richie delivered Rosie around four,' Spike said. 'I been here since.'

'You haven't been trying on my clothes, have you?'

'I wanted to,' Spike said. 'But there was a size problem.'

'God, I hope so,' I said.

'Tell me about LA,' Spike said.

Which I did. By the time I got through, we had opened a second bottle of Riesling and my coherence was becoming endangered.

'Erin was a hooker,' Spike said.

'Yes. I suppose that's why she pretended that Misty was just her assistant. The rigmarole with names. Keep her origins a mystery.'

'She seems to keep getting rescued by men and being rebuilt. First the pimp ...'

'Gerard,' I said.

'Then Buddy Bollen.'

'She married Gerard,' I said.

'And she lives with Buddy?'

I nodded.

'How's the pimp?' Spike said.

'What's he like?'

'Yeah.'

'What you'd expect. Self-important. Soulless. Filled with contempt for women. Except that he claims still to be in love with Erin. It doesn't fit.'

'Things don't,' Spike said.

'Be easier if they did,' I said.

'But boring,' Spike said.

'Still a man who exploits women for money,' I said.

'Not all whores are exploited,' Spike said.

I was a woman. I knew the official woman's view of prostitution. I started to say it.

'It's not a victimless crime,' I said. 'The whores are victims.'

'Some,' Spike said. 'Perhaps many. Nobody likes giving BJs at truck stops. But you've known whores who liked being whores.'

I drank some wine. I looked at Rosie. She appeared agnostic about the question.

'I ... yes. I have,' I said. 'Especially the high-end hookers. They like the good clothes, the nice restaurants, the luxury hotels, the good money. Hell, they like the sex. Don't tell anyone in Cambridge I said that. I may have to go there someday.'

'Maybe Erin liked it,' Spike said. 'Given the way you describe her situation with Buddy, maybe she still does.'

'Maybe,' I said.

'Maybe the pimp really does love her,' Spike said.

'Maybe.'

'And while we're speaking the unspeakable, maybe you did the nasty again with Tony Gault.'

'It wasn't nasty,' I said. 'You're just jealous.'

'I only met him once when he was in Boston,' Spike said.

'You know how you are,' I said.

Spike grinned.

'I know how both of us are,' he said. 'You're easy.'

'I am not easy,' I said. 'But I'm fun.'

23

Paradise, Massachusetts, in late November was the perfect reentry fix from Southern California. It was gray. Snow was spitting. And the wind off the Atlantic was persistent. I parked in the lot next to the Paradise police station and went in to see the chief.

'Back from California,' I said. 'Ready to compare notes.'

'Do you eat lunch?' Jesse said.

'I do.'

'Me too,' Jesse Stone said. 'Let's compare notes over it.'

'That would be very nice,' I said.

We walked together through Paradise to a restaurant called Daisy's. The owner was a strapping woman with humorous eyes. Jesse introduced us. She showed us to a table, put two menus down, and left.

'Sandwiches are good here,' Jesse said. 'They bake their own bread.'

I ordered tunafish on light rye. He ordered a lobster club on anadama bread. We both had mango iced tea.

'How's Cronjager?' Jesse said.

'Good. He seems like a good man.'

'He is. Did you meet Elaine?'

'Yes. Smart woman.'

'She is,' Jesse said. 'Good woman, too.'

'It's like she's the real captain,' I said.

Jesse nodded.

'She thinks so, and Cronjager lets her. How's he look?'

'Mature, gray hair, healthy.'

'Hair was gray when I knew him,' Jesse said. 'What do you know?'

'Me first?' I said.

He nodded. I told him what I knew about Erin and Misty. Jesse listened quietly. While I talked he sipped his iced tea occasionally and didn't eat his sandwich.

'You think Gerard actually loves her?' Jesse said when I finished.

'I think he thinks he does,' I said.

Jesse nodded.

'Hard to know the difference sometimes,' he said.

I took a ladylike little bite of my sandwich and looked at him for a moment while I chewed it. When people are quiet there's a tendency to think that there is more to them than there seems to be. Usually you're wrong. But sometimes there is.

'Pimps don't usually love women,' I said.

'No,' Jesse said. 'They don't. But sometimes the women think they do, and sometimes the pimps think they do, too.'

'Believe their own con,' I said.

'Uh-huh.'

'So do you think he flew out here in a jealous rage and killed Misty to punish Erin for leaving him?'

'Seems a reach,' Jesse said.

'He claims to be a martial-arts master.'

'So he would probably know how to snap a neck,' Jesse said. 'If he ever used it for real.'

'Not just mat exercises?'

'For real is different,' Jesse said.

'Do you know anything?' I said.

'Very little,' Jesse said. 'But I'm used to it. Fingerprints are meaningless. Everybody at SeaChase used the gym, even Buddy. Plus the people who installed it, cleaned it.'

'Alibis?'

'Not many. Most people at SeaChase were alone during the time when Erin could have died. A few off-duty employees were with significant others. But nobody has an ironclad alibi. Including you.'

'Am I a suspect?' I said.

'No.'

'Any suspects?'

'No.'

'How do you want to use what I've learned?' I said.

'It's your stuff,' he said. 'How do you want to use it?'

Jesse took his first bite of sandwich. I thought for a minute while he chewed.

'I think you should bring her in and break it to her without saying where it came from,' I said.

'If I bring Erin in, Buddy will come, too,' Jesse said.

'And no doubt a lawyer.'

'No doubt,' Jesse said. 'You want to be there?'

'Yes.'

'But you don't want to take credit for blowing her cover?'

'No.'

'She hired you to find out who killed Misty; what you're doing is what you were hired to do,' Jesse said.

'Even if she killed her sister?' I said.

'You think she did?'

'It doesn't seem like she would,' I said. 'Their history is Erin taking care of Misty.'

Jesse nodded.

'Be interesting to see what you'd do if she did,' Jesse said.

'She hired me to find the killer,' I said.

Jesse said 'Yes' and took another bite of his sandwich.

'Do you know anything else?' I said. 'If not useful, at least interesting?'

Jesse chewed carefully and swallowed and drank some tea.

'Talked with Roy Linden,' Jesse said.

'The baseball coach?' I said.

'Yeah.'

'What did you talk about?'

'He and I knew some of the same people,' Jesse said. 'We talked about that and after a while we talked about Erin.'

'What did he say?'

'Well, he's got his official position,' Jesse said.

'Which is that Erin will be a great major-league baseball player,' I said.

'Um-hmm,' Jesse said.

'But?'

Jesse shook his head.

'She won't,' I said.

'Roy doesn't think so,' Jesse said.

'Because?'

'She won't hit major-league pitching,' Jesse said.

'But she can play the field?'

'Probably. He thinks she can probably run down a lot of balls in center field and probably catch most of them. She's got a mediocre arm, but plenty of big-league outfielders do. She can probably run the bases pretty good.'

'But she won't hit?' I said.

'Roy doesn't say so, but that's what he thinks.'

'How long has he been coaching her?'

'Since she's been with Buddy,' Jesse said.

'So this is not a new plan,' I said.

Jesse shook his head.

'How do you know people that Roy Linden knows?'

'We both played in the Pacific Coast League,' Jesse said.

'Baseball?'

'Yep.'

'Did you ever play anywhere, like, you know, a place I'd have heard of?'

'Played at Albuquerque,' Jesse said. 'Triple A.'

'What's Triple A?'

'One level short of the major leagues,' Jesse said.

'But you didn't make the major leagues?'

'Hurt my shoulder, couldn't throw anymore,' he said. 'I was a shortstop.'

'Oh, what a shame,' I said. 'Do you miss it?'

'Yes.'

'If you hadn't gotten hurt, would you have made the big leagues?'

'Yes.'

'You keep a baseball glove in your office.'

'I play in the town softball league.'

'So you can still play softball.'

'I can throw well enough for that,' Jesse said.

'Maybe you should go with me to watch Erin train with Roy Linden. Every morning. Taft University.'

'What would that tell us?'

'I don't know,' I said. 'But it would be good to know what you thought of her chances.'

'And it's always better to know than not know,' Jesse said.

'I think so,' I said.

'And you're fun to be with,' Jesse said.

I smiled at him.

'You have no idea,' I said.
He raised his eyebrows.
'Maybe I do,' he said.
My face felt a little warm. I hadn't meant to say that. The waitress came and refilled our iced-tea glasses. I put some Equal into my iced tea and sipped some. Jesse looked at me carefully. He probably looked at everything that way. Still, I was aware that I had dressed very thoughtfully when I decided to come see him. Gray jeans, a white shirt with big cuffs, worn with the shirttails out, a black velveteen jacket, and short boots with heels that should have been higher, but, being a detective, I felt that I needed the capacity for sudden mobility. Still, it was a great look, even without the stiletto heels, because it could be considered dressing up, or dressing down. I felt good about it.
'Was that before, it must have been, before you became a cop, that you got hurt?'
'Yes.'
'So,' I said, 'how did you end up here?'
'My marriage went south. I drank too much. Got fired.'
'By Captain Cronjager,' I said. 'Why did you come here?'
'They're the ones would have me,' Jesse said.
'The drinking is under control?' I said.
Why was that my business?
'At the moment.'
'And you're divorced?'
'More or less,' Jesse said. 'But we're giving it another try.'
'She move back in?' I said.
Why was that *my business?*
Jesse smiled. 'She lives in Boston,' he said. 'We have sleepovers.'
'How's that going?' I said.
'Day at a time.'
'I'm divorced, too,' I said.
Why was that his business?
'Neat and clean?'
'I guess,' I said. 'He's remarried.'
'But?' Jesse said.
'We're not fully, ah, disengaged, I guess.'
He nodded.

'Children?' I said.
'No.'
'Me either.'
It was like we were filling out each other's résumé: Which side of the bed do you prefer? How do you like your eggs in the morning? Do you sleep in the nude?
'I have a dog,' I said.
Jesse nodded.
'I like dogs,' he said.

24

Erin was not happy to be in the Paradise police station. Nor did she seem particularly happy to see me there. But Erin, now that I thought about it, never seemed particularly happy anyway. Buddy was with her, and two lawyers. The lead lawyer was a large man with a red face. His associate was a thoughtful-looking woman, somewhat younger than he.

'I see no reason why I had to come down here,' Erin said as she came into the conference room, which was big enough to accommodate the anticipated group. Jesse rose when they entered, offered seats to everyone, and sat down at his end of the conference table.

'I'm Jesse Stone,' Jesse said to the two lawyers. 'This is Sunny Randall. I assume you know who each of us is.'

'We do,' the male lawyer said.

The lawyers introduced themselves. The man's name was Thomas Hammer. His associate was Bebe Ablon.

'You are not under arrest,' Jesse said to Erin. 'Nor are you accused of a crime.'

'So, I'm here because you're a star fucker, right?'

'Depends on the star,' Jesse said. 'We just need to clear up a few points.'

'What's she doing here?' Erin said.

'You have employed Ms. Randall. She and I have a common goal,' Jesse said. 'I am being courteous.'

Bebe Ablon leaned over and murmured something to Hammer. He nodded.

'Let's hear Chief Stone for a bit,' Hammer said.

'Sure, but don't tell me he's not getting his rocks off doing this,' Erin said. 'Having a few beers with the boys later and telling them about it.'

Jesse nodded.

'That is, of course, the thrilling part of my job,' he said. 'But before I do that, can you tell me who Ethel Boverini is?'

Erin froze, staring at Jesse. Her eyes fluttered for a moment, as if she wanted to look at her lawyers, or Buddy, or all three. Then she toughened.

'I don't know,' she said.

'Edith Boverini?' Jesse said.

'I don't know.'

'You don't know if you know them or you don't know if you know?'

'I don't know. Why are you asking me this stuff?'

'So I can tell the boys later,' Jesse said. 'Is Misty Tyler your sister?'

'I … I don't know.'

'Are you married to a man named Gerard Basgall?'

Erin was buckling. She sagged in her chair. Her face was down. She was beginning to cry. She put her hands to her face.

'Stop asking me these questions,' Erin said. 'Stop it.'

'Jesse, for crissake,' Buddy said. 'What's wrong with you?'

Bebe put her hand on Buddy's arm.

'Chief Stone,' Hammer said, 'could we have a few minutes alone with Ms. Flint?'

'Sure,' Jesse said.

Again, Bebe whispered something to Hammer. He nodded.

'Buddy,' Hammer said. 'If you don't mind, perhaps you and Ms. Randall could leave us as well.'

'I'm not going anywhere,' Buddy said. 'I'm paying you, pal. You don't tell me what to do.'

Erin was crying hard now.

'Get out of here,' Erin said. 'Everybody get the fuck out of here.'

'You going to be all right, Erin?' Buddy said.

'Get the fuck out,' Erin gasped, the words running together between spurts of crying.

It was probably real. I'd seen no sign that she could act well enough to fake it. Buddy and Jesse and I stood and left Erin alone in the conference room with her lawyers.

We sat in Jesse's office.

'What the fuck is going on, Stone?' Buddy said.

'Just looking for clues,' Jesse said.

His glove was still on the top of the file cabinet. There was no picture of the divorced wife displayed. That was heartening.

'So what's all this shit about Bonfoolgio and Gerard and sisters and crap?'

'We'll eventually get that cleared up with Erin,' Jesse said.

'I want it cleared up with me,' Buddy said.

'Don't blame you,' Jesse said.

'So? What about it?'

'We'll clear it up with Erin,' Jesse said. 'Then you and she can discuss it.'

'Listen, Stone. I own Erin Flint. I own her career. I get what I want. And right now I want an explanation.'

'How'd you meet Erin?' Jesse said.

'Goddamn it, don't you presume to question me. Where'd you dig up all this shit?'

Jesse shook his head.

'We might as well get this clear now,' I said. 'I got this information. Erin's real name is Ethel Boverini. Misty is her younger sister, Edith. When she was eighteen, Erin married a man in Los Angeles County named Gerard Basgall.'

'You found this out?'

'Yes.'

'You're supposed to be working for us,' Buddy said.

'I am,' I said. 'You hired me to find out who killed Misty. I'm trying to do that.'

'By investigating Erin?'

'Everybody,' I said. 'I'm not some one-woman crime lab. I can't solve your crime if I don't know what there is to know about the people involved.'

'You, little lady, are fucking fired as of fucking now,' Buddy said.

'Little lady,' Jesse murmured.

I grinned at him for a moment.

'You didn't hire me,' I said. 'You can't fire me.'

'Who you think's been paying you?'

'The checks so far have been signed by Erin Flint,' I said.

'Where do you think she gets the money?'

'Don't know,' I said. 'Don't care.'

'Listen, bitch …' Buddy started.

'Buddy,' Jesse said.

He didn't raise his voice, but there was suddenly a little glitter of ice in it.

Buddy stared at him. He looked a little uncertain, which, for Buddy, would have been a rare experience.

'You become abusive and I will have to restrain you.'

'Me?'

'Maybe even slap you in a cell for the night. And who knows, it's even possible that during the night you would fall in your cell and hurt yourself.'

'Jesus Christ, are you threatening me?' Buddy said.

Jesse looked at me.

'What do you think, little lady?' he said. 'Was that a threat?'

I smiled and nodded slowly. Buddy stared at both of us. There was a knock on the office door and Hammer stuck his head in.

'Ms. Flint is prepared to talk with you now,' he said.

25

Erin's eyes were puffy and her face was red, but she wasn't crying. Bebe Ablon sat beside her with a hand resting on Erin's forearm. Hammer went to the side of the room and stood against the wall behind Erin and folded his arms.

'If we could,' Hammer said, 'we'd like Ms. Flint to say her say without interruption. If there are questions, we'd greatly appreciate it if you'd wait until she's had her say.'

Jesse had apparently cowed Buddy for the moment. None of us said anything. Erin studied her hands, which she had folded on the tabletop in front of her. Bebe patted her arm and nodded.

'My real name is Ethel Boverini,' Erin said softly. 'My sister was Edith Boverini, but she used the name Misty Tyler.'

Buddy opened his mouth and looked at Hammer. Hammer put his finger to his lips and Buddy didn't speak.

'When I was eighteen,' Erin went on, 'after my mother died, I married a man named Gerard Basgall. We have never formally divorced. Edith was seventeen. We went to live with Gerard and he took care of us.'

Erin stopped and took in some deep breaths. Bebe patted her forearm.

'The three of us started a business,' Erin said.

She sounded short of breath.

'Gerard would set us up… He had a connection at a nice hotel and we'd go there with men… Gerard made sure they were nice… And he'd always stay around and make sure we were okay… Some men like young girls … and after a while we started going to different hotels … always upper-class … and we got to meet a lot of important movie people … and then Gerard hired some more girls and the business got to be pretty big … and me and Edith only did the special clients.'

'When did you become Erin Flint?' Hammer said gently from his place against the wall.

'Gerard changed our names,' Erin said. 'Right when we first went with him.'

'And why did you use different names?' Hammer said.

'I don't know. Some guys liked that we were sisters, you know? Both at the same time. Some guys, I guess, didn't. So we had different names. Gerard told us.'

'And when did you, ah, leave Gerard?' Hammer said.

'When I met Buddy.'

Everyone was quiet. Erin kept studying her hands.

'Questions?' Hammer said.

Bebe had stopped patting Erin's forearm, but her hand still rested there.

'How did you meet Buddy?' I said.

'Hotel,' Erin said with no inflection and without raising her head.

'Hey,' Buddy said.

'Everybody knows everything, Buddy,' Erin said.

'Well, if the fucking media gets it,' Buddy said, 'your career is fucking history.'

'That's not necessarily going to happen,' Hammer said. 'And if it did, it wouldn't necessarily ruin anyone's career.'

'You shut the fuck up,' Buddy said. 'You and her' – Buddy pointed his chin at Bebe – 'are fucking fired, as of right now.'

Hammer looked a little tired. If anything, Bebe looked a little amused. I wondered how many times Buddy had fired them before.

'I bring you down here to protect us, for crissake,' Buddy said, 'and you got her blabbing her whole goddamned whore history.'

'You knew I was a whore, Buddy,' Erin said softly.

For a moment I almost liked her.

'Shut up,' Buddy said.

'Buddy,' I said.

'You shut up, too,' Buddy said.

'Buddy,' I said. 'Stop having a tantrum. This isn't some cute business ploy that didn't work. This is a homicide investigation. There are no secrets.'

'Not with you on the fucking job,' Buddy said.

'I'm a detective. DNA and fingerprints and powder traces are nice,' I said. 'But most clues are human, they have to do with who people are and where they've been. Erin, you want me to find out who killed Misty. If you don't want that, say so now. Because if I stay on, I'll keep doing what I do.'

'Bullshit,' Buddy said.

Hammer said, 'Let's make this decision together, Buddy. Not right now, right here.'

Buddy started to brush him off, and stopped, and looked at him, and nodded slowly.

'Okay,' Buddy said. 'Okay.'

Jesse was looking at Erin. Her face was gray now, and her head hung, and her shoulders slumped.

'There are a lot more questions we will have to ask,' he said to her. 'But we don't have to ask them now.'

He smiled at Erin.

'Why don't you go home and have a drink?'

She looked up at him for a moment and nodded her head.

'Yes,' she said.

'Let's get the fuck outta here,' Buddy said, and headed for the door. Erin and the two lawyers followed. The lawyers shook hands with me and Jesse as they left. Hammer gave us both a card.

'That was kind of you,' I said to Jesse when we were alone.

He grinned.

'How'd you like to be Buddy Bollen's lawyer?' Jesse said.

'They were better than many,' I said.

'Yes. That woman lawyer,' Jesse said, 'Bebe. Didn't say a single thing I could hear.'

'I know.'

'She was quiet and thoughtful,' Jesse said.

'Not a bad thing in a lawyer,' I said.

'I wonder how she got through law school,' Jesse said.

26

Jesse and I went to watch Erin work out in the cage at Taft. She was wearing Adidas spikes, a black tank top, gray shorts, and a black adjustable baseball cap worn backward. Roy Linden was leaning on the edge of the batting cage, his chin on his folded forearms. A different college kid was pitching. Two of Buddy's security guys stood near the batting cage.

'I spent about two hours with her Monday,' Jesse said.

Erin hit the ball very hard into the billowing field house net. She glanced triumphantly at Roy Linden.

'Good,' Roy Linden said. 'Nice.'

'Out of any park,' Erin said.

'It's what happens,' Roy Linden said, 'you stay nice and compact.'

'How was she?' I said.

'Recovered.'

'Erin Flint again?' I said.

'Uh-huh.'

Erin hit a ball that bounced weakly toward the pitcher.

'Nice and easy,' Roy Linden said, 'short swing. Bottom hand leads, top hand follows.'

'Tell him to throw it higher,' Erin said.

'If you don't like a pitch, Erin,' Linden said, 'just lay off it.'

'And do what?' she said. 'Just stand here?'

'She does seem her old self,' I said to Jesse.

'Buddy wasn't there,' Jesse said. 'Just her and the woman lawyer.'

Erin hit the ball hard again.

'Excellent,' Roy Linden said. 'Head right on it. Excellent.'

'She doesn't know anyone who would want to hurt Misty. She doesn't have any idea who might have done it. She still thinks it was meant to be her, trying to stop her from playing big-league ball.'

'Just stand in the box,' Linden said to Erin. 'Don't swing. I just want you to pick up his release point.'

'Just stand here?'

'Tell me,' Linden said, 'when he releases the ball.'

'That's boring,' she said.

'You bet,' Linden said.

'She have any thought about who it might be that's trying to stop her?'

'The old boys' network,' Jesse said.

I nodded.

'You need to see it sooner,' Roy Linden was saying. 'Focus. Try to see the ball leaving his hand.'

'For crissake, Roy, as long as I see it, what difference?'

Linden's calm never faltered.

'Sooner you see it, Erin, longer you've got to decide what pitch it is and whether to swing.'

Jesse was staring at the pitcher as we talked. I realized he was watching for the release point, too.

'Buddy sent her to college, her and Misty. It was probably her happiest time.'

'She tell you that?' I said.

Jesse smiled and shook his head.

Erin said, 'There.'

'Slow,' Jesse said. 'She needs to see it sooner.'

'So why do you say she was happy in college?'

'Way she talked,' Jesse said.

He still looked at the pitcher and nodded when the pitcher released the ball. I doubt that he was aware of it.

'She played volleyball, softball. Ran track.'

'Dated?' I said.

'I gathered, not too much,' Jesse said. 'She was older than most of the college boys, and looked like she looks. Most of them were probably scared to ask her out.'

'Plus she was already with Buddy,' I said.

Jesse nodded briefly as the pitcher released the ball. His nod was still ahead of Erin's recognition.

'I'm not sure faithful is part of their deal,' Jesse said.

'It might be part of the deal,' I said, 'but I don't think either of them would be ruled by it.'

'Whaddya throw?' Roy Linden yelled out to the college kid pitching.

'Fastball, curve,' the kid said. 'Got a circle change but I can't locate it.'

'Throw what you got,' Linden said. 'Mix them up. I don't care about location. I want her to see the rotation.'

'It still bothers me,' I said, 'that the two girls concealed their relationship.'

Jesse nodded, watching the pitcher.

'They were still doing it,' I said, 'even after Misty died. Erin was still not admitting that they were sisters.'

'They lived in a culture of denial,' Jesse said.

'I just see the ball,' Erin said.

'You'll get it, keep focused on the release point, see how the ball rotates when he lets it go.'

'I don't see anything,' Erin said.

'Focus,' Linden said.

'Culture of denial?' I said to Jesse. 'Are you sure you're a cop?'

'God made her look like she does,' Jesse said. 'To live up to that, she has to deny everything else.'

'Even her sister?'

'Sister knows,' Jesse said.

'But pretending she's not your sister doesn't make her not know,' I said.

'Why they call it denial,' Jesse said.
I looked at him for a while. He glanced at me.
'I've done shrink time,' he said.
'Ex-wife?' I said.
'Some.'
'I've done it, too,' I said.
'Ex-husband?'
'Some.'
Jesse smiled.
'How's it working?' he said.
'I'm a lot better than I would be without it,' I said.
Jesse nodded.
We sat silently for a time. It wasn't an uncomfortable silence. We seemed to be mutually at ease with our therapies and each other. As we sat, Erin dropped her bat and walked out of the batting cage.
'I don't see any fucking spin,' she said. 'And I don't think you do.'
'Spring training doesn't start till March,' Roy Linden said. 'We got time.'
'Bullshit,' Erin said and walked away toward the locker room.
The two security guys walked along after her, looking in all directions, staying close. Roy Linden waved at us and walked out of the gym. Jesse and I were alone in the stands.
'Is there a spin?' I said.
'Yeah. Helps you recognize what the pitch will be.'
'Could you see it?'
'I could if I were hitting,' Jesse said. 'Not from here.'
The gym was empty. The amount of unoccupied space around us underscored how close we were sitting. The silence was substantial.
'What was the problem with you and your husband?' Jesse said.
'I'm still figuring that out,' I said. 'But one of them was me.'
'Hard to imagine,' Jesse said.
'Think how I feel,' I said.
We were quiet again.
Without looking at me Jesse said, 'Jenn cheated on me.'
'Ouch,' I said.
Jesse nodded.
'More than once?' I said.

'Many more.'

'Hard to trust her now?' I said.

'Yes.'

More quiet, both of us surveying the empty gym.

'Richie has remarried,' I said.

'Ouch,' Jesse said.

I nodded. Somewhere out of sight in the gym, a door opened and closed. The sound only underscored the silence. I was aware of my clothes and of myself inside them.

'I feel a little tense,' I said.

'Me too,' Jesse said.

'But I like it,' I said.

'Me too,' Jesse said.

We looked at each other. There was no uneasiness between us and no challenge. We just looked at each other, seeing what was there.

'I don't know exactly what it means,' I said.

'No,' Jesse said. 'But it means something.'

'We might as well follow it,' I said. 'See where it goes.'

'No rush,' Jesse said.

'And your ex-wife?' I said.

'I don't know,' Jesse said.

'Well,' I said after a time. 'I guess we'll probably find that out, too.'

27

I sat with Richie's Uncle Felix in the backseat of a silver Mercedes sedan parked off of Soldier's Field Road in Brighton and looked at the Charles River. Outside the car, Felix's driver leaned on the left-front fender and smoked a cigarette.

I said, 'Thanks for seeing me, Felix.'

'I like you, Sunny, even if you ain't with Richie,' Felix said.

He had a voice like Darth Vader. I wanted to ask him how he liked Richie's new wife.

'How is Richie?' I said.

'He's fine,' Felix said.

Felix wasn't here to talk about Richie. With his brother Desmond, my former father-in-law, Felix ran the Irish Mob in Boston. Desmond did the corporate planning. Felix enforced it. He was quite brutal, but there was in him some strange courtliness and, despite myself, I liked him.

'I was talking with my father,' I said. 'About a case I'm on.'

Felix nodded his massive gray head. My father and he had met in the course of their duties.

'He said money often connects with, ah, mobsters.'

'Like me,' Felix said.

'Nobody is exactly like you, Felix.'

He nodded.

'Do you know a man named Buddy Bollen?' I said.

'Heard of him,' Felix said.

He sat with his thick hands folded over his round, hard stomach. They rose and fell slightly as he breathed. Otherwise, he didn't move.

'What can you tell me about him?'

'He's a player,' Felix said.

'Which means?'

'Means he makes a lot of money and spends a lot and don't mind cutting corners. Means when he wants to cut corners he don't mind dealing with guys like me and Desmond.'

'So have you done any business?'

'Me and Desmond? No. I was just using a, ah, figure of speech.'

'But you might know somebody he did business with?'

'I might find out,' Felix said. 'Whaddya want to know?'

'Anything,' I said. 'A woman was murdered in his house and I'm trying to find out who did it.'

'I'll ask around,' Felix said. 'Anybody give you trouble?'

'Like what?' I said.

'Witness knows something won't tell you,' Felix said. 'I could help with that.'

I smiled.

'No, not at the moment. Thank you, Felix.'

He nodded, looking out at the bright, gray river. I didn't say anything. Neither did he. After a time, Felix turned and looked at me. It had weight to it. It was as if I could feel his stare.

'How you doing, Sunny?'

'Good,' I said. 'Good.'

'You still got Rosie?' he said.

'Yes.'

'Goddamnedest dog I ever seen,' Felix said. 'Richie used to have her sometimes in the tavern.'

'She still visits him,' I said. 'Every week.'

Felix nodded. He looked out the window at the river again and was quiet.

After a time, and still looking at the river, Felix said, 'Richie's gonna have a kid.'

It was difficult to breathe.

I managed to say, 'Oh?'

'Wife's pregnant,' Felix said. 'Four months.'

'I didn't know.'

I felt as if I had frozen solid. Felix's cavernous voice seemed remote.

'They know what?' I said. My voice sounded like a distant squeak to me.

'Boy,' Felix said from somewhere.

I didn't say anything. Felix put his hand on my thigh and patted me for a moment.

'Now you know,' he said.

I nodded and got out of the car. The driver flipped his cigarette and stepped quickly to hold the door.

'Thank you, Felix,' I said.

'I'll ask around,' he said. 'Get back to you.'

I stepped away. The driver closed the door. I walked to my own car and got in and closed the door. I sat for a moment, trying to breathe. Beside me the Mercedes pulled out of the parking area and out onto Soldier's Field Road. I watched it briefly in the rearview mirror as it headed west toward Newton, and then my vision blurred and I couldn't see much of anything.

28

Spike and I tried to have dinner together every Tuesday night when we could. Tonight we were having whole-wheat spaghetti with meatballs, cooked by Spike, and some Kendall Jackson Riesling, bought by me. Rosie sat beside me on my extra-wide chair, and Spike put a precooled meatball on a saucer in front of her. Rosie ate it. I drank some of my wine.

'One of the things in being a detective,' I said, 'is you learn a lot of stuff.'

'Which means,' Spike said, 'that if you do it for a while, you know a lot of stuff.'

'I guess,' I said.

I drank some more wine. Kendall Jackson Riesling was my favorite.

'So what did you learn today?' Spike said.

He wasn't drinking wine. He had Jack Daniel's on the rocks. Rosie watched us beadily. There was no way to predict from whence another meatball might appear.

'I've been thinking about Erin Flint,' I said.

'Lot of people do,' Spike said.

'She's pathetic,' I said.

I drank some wine.

'She's high camp.'

'You like her?' I said.

My wineglass was empty. I refilled it.

'I'm usually focused on the leading man,' Spike said. 'What's so pathetic?'

I drank some wine.

'She ...'

I drank a little more wine and thought about it.

'She is a great physical specimen,' I said. 'Very athletic. Very beautiful. She's a big star. She makes a ton of money. She may become the first woman to play major-league baseball.'

I drank some wine.

'And as far as I can see, she is not happy for one minute during the day,' I said. 'What a shame.'

'I've seen her movies,' Spike said. 'Thus proving that I really am gay.'

'She has no acting talent,' I said.

'None,' Spike said. 'So where's that leave her?'

'It leaves her with only two things she can rely on,' I said. 'Her looks and the kindness of rich men.'

'And when one goes,' Spike said, 'the other goes.'

Spike turned the short whiskey glass slowly around on the tabletop. His hands were thick. Rosie watched him rotate his glass with the blank avidity of a Peeping Tom.

'So there's nothing to fall back on,' I said.

Spike shook his head.

'She acts with her appearance,' he said. 'When her appearance is no longer compelling ...'

He shrugged.

'And no one loves her,' I said.

'Buddy?'

'No, I hardly think so.'

'Sister's dead,' Spike said. 'Anybody else?'

I shook my head.

'There's a pimp in LA,' I said. 'Claims he loves her.'

I looked at him.

'Not too consoling,' Spike said.

'No.'

Spike sipped a small sip of Jack Daniel's. He watched as I poured more wine for myself.

'Poor little rich girl,' Spike said.

'When I saw her naked, in the women's locker room, I thought that I would give five years off my life to look like that.'

'Beauty doesn't buy happiness?' Spike said.

'I know it's a cliché, but seeing it close-up – rich, beautiful, and unhappy – it doesn't,' I said.

'That's been true for me, too,' Spike said.

'You have to have something – a skill, a talent – that's yours, that can't be taken from you.'

'Or a someone,' Spike said.

I nodded. I was a little drunk. I felt like I wanted to be more drunk. Rosie shifted her black, almond-eyed stare onto me. She had a gaze like a Modigliani painting.

'Or someone,' I said.

I patted Rosie's head softly. My eyes began to fill. God, I was going to cry. Spike was watching me. I dropped my head. I tried deep breaths to forestall it, but it wasn't working. My deep breaths were shaky.

'Let her rip, honey,' Spike said. 'Who would you rather cry with than me?'

'I don't want to scare Rosie,' I said.

I had trouble getting the words out.

'Sunny,' Spike said, 'while the potential for meatballs exists, Rosie won't care if you have an extended case of demonic possession.'

'I know,' I said.

And the crying came. Face in hands, shoulders shaking. Boo hoo.

Spike sat quietly, sipping his Jack Daniel's, watching me. Rosie remained calm. The crying lasted maybe five minutes, which is a long time to cry. Then I was quiet for a while longer, getting my breathing under control.

'Richie's having a baby,' I said finally.

'Whoops,' Spike said.

I nodded. We sat. I drank some wine.

'It's never over till it's over,' Spike said after a while. 'I've always said that.'

I shrugged, looking in my glass at the still surface of my wine.

'And now it's over,' Spike said.

'I guess,' I said.

29

Jesse parked his car by the lighthouse at the end of Stiles Island. We could look west at the harbor, and east at the open Atlantic. It was the first of December, and spitting snow. Jesse left the motor running so we could have some heat. The wipers moved intermittently on the windshield. There was something lovely-looking about the juxtaposition of small snow and gray ocean.

'Want to go over it?' Jesse said.

'I guess,' I said.

'Suspects?'

'Not because I have evidence,' I said, 'just a list of people I can't rule out.'

'Me too,' Jesse said.

'Erin,' I said.

Jesse nodded.

'Buddy,' I said.

Nod.

'Gerard.'

'The LA pimp,' Jesse said.

I nodded.

'And person or persons unknown,' I said.

'I got them, too,' Jesse said. 'Anyone else?'

'Not without getting silly,' I said. 'I mean, the baseball guy could have done it; or Robbie, her trainer; or any of the security guys, except those with an alibi; and the cook; and a couple of maids ...'

'And the first three hundred names in the Paradise phone book,' Jesse said.

'It doesn't mean that one of them didn't do it,' I said.

'We'll save them for when we get desperate,' Jesse said.

I smiled. 'Like when you lose your keys,' I said, 'and if you can't find them for long enough, you end up looking in the refrigerator or the toilet tank.'

He nodded.

'Gerard is a karate guy,' I said.

'Three thousand miles away,' Jesse said.

'Six hours,' I said.

We both sat quietly for a time, watching the snowflakes disappear on the dull, uneasy water.

'Do you think Erin could have done it?' I said after a time.

'She's big and strong,' Jesse said.

'She's probably more capable than Buddy,' I said. 'When you think of it.'

'Strength wouldn't be an issue,' Jesse said, 'if there was a combination of events.'

'Like Misty turned her head left at the precise moment someone was twisting it right?'

'Something like that,' Jesse said.

'The only other thing is, my father suggested that somebody like Buddy, all that money, might have some sort of Mob connection.'

Jesse nodded.

'This is in confidence,' I said.

'Sure,' Jesse said.

'My ex-husband's uncle is a figure in organized crime in Boston.'

'Felix Burke,' Jesse said.

'Goddamn you,' I said. 'Have I no secrets?'

'Maybe we'll find that out someday.'

I paused for a minute. *What did that mean?*

'Anyway,' I said. 'Felix is going to look into Buddy's connections, if any, and let me know.'

'Still family,' Jesse said.

'Felix is a thug and a stone killer,' I said. 'But we somehow like each other.'

'Until you cross him,' Jesse said.

'I'll try not to.'

There was no movement in the harbor. There was no wind and the water was almost still. No boats. No gulls. Only the insignificant fall of the thin snow. Jesse's hands were quiet on the steering wheel; mine were folded in my lap. We both looked at the ocean as if there were something to see. Neither of us spoke.

Finally I said, 'How is it going with your ex?'

Jesse turned and looked at me thoughtfully for a long time.

'Mediocre,' he said after a while.

'I thought it was going well,' I said.

He shrugged. 'It was,' he said. 'Now it's not.'

'I'm sorry,' I said. 'Would you like to talk about it?'

'No,' he said. 'Yes.'

I waited.

'The truth is, of course, she was the only person I could ever really talk to about this sort of thing and …'

He shrugged. I leaned a little toward him, but I didn't say anything.

'I would like to talk about it,' he said after a while.

He turned his head and looked at me for the first time.

'I'd like to talk about it with you,' he said. 'But not now. Not yet.'

'When the time comes,' I said. 'You can tell me your story, and I'll tell you mine.'

Jesse smiled at me. 'Misery loves company,' he said.

The snowfall had increased. A single herring gull drifted through the snow squall, circling down above the car, hoping perhaps for a discarded french fry. It landed beside the car and hopped around, cocking its head. It reminded me of Rosie, with its expressionless black eyes and its intensity. There were no french fries, nor popcorn, nor orange peels, nor bread crumbs. After a time, the gull flew away into the falling snow.

30

Rosie and I met Felix and another man in the parking lot of a Dunkin' Donuts in Andrews Square. Felix sat behind the wheel, the other man in the front with him. Rosie and I got into the backseat. As soon as we got in I unhooked Rosie's leash and she jumped into the front, jostling the passenger in the process, and squirmed onto Felix's lap.

The passenger said, 'What the fuck?'

'It's Rosie,' Felix said. 'I like Rosie.'

Rosie's tail thump-thumped against Felix's wide rib cage. He patted her. The passenger looked as if he wasn't a dog person. But, like most of the world, he preferred not to argue with Felix.

'She's Sunny,' Felix said. 'He's Eddie. He's going to tell you what he knows about Buddy Bollen.'

Eddie was small and pale-skinned. He had on a navy watch cap and a pea jacket.

'She don't say where she got this,' Eddie said.

'No,' Felix said.

'And he doesn't make things up,' I said.

'Eddie ain't smart enough to make things up,' Felix said.

'Hey,' Eddie said.

Felix made a sound that I knew was his version of laughing.

'Tell her what you know,' Felix said.

Having squeezed into place behind the steering wheel, Rosie had settled into Felix's lap. Felix patted her. Eddie looked straight ahead at the front door of the Dunkin' Donuts and began to talk.

'Guy named Moon Monaghan,' he said. 'Used to be a collector for a shark named Patsy Lang. Then one day Patsy was gone and Moon was in charge.'

'What happened to Patsy?' I said.

Eddie shrugged. 'Something,' he said. 'As soon as he took over, Moon juiced the whole fucking shylock thing, ya know? Loaned out more money, collected more vig. Nobody ever didn't pay Moon. After a while, he's pulling in so much cash he's trying to find places to store it. He had cash in one of them public warehouse storage lockers for a while, looking for ways to wash it.'

'And you know this how?' I said.

Rosie had flipped over on Felix's lap with her feet sticking up and her tongue lolling out while Felix rubbed her stomach.

Eddie shrugged again and shook his head.

'So Moon's got a cousin,' he said, 'shyster named Arlo Delaney. In LA. And Arlo hooks him up with a couple dudes that finance pictures.'

'Names?' I said.

Eddie shook his head, still staring straight ahead at the donut shop.

'Ran a company called Hollywood Investment Team. They're looking for cash. Moon's looking for something besides a storage locker, ya know, for his cash.'

Eddie spread his hands.

'Love at first sight,' he said. 'Ya know?'

Rosie had fallen asleep in Felix's lap. I could hear her soft snoring. Felix had stopped patting her and was simply resting his massive hand on her pink stomach.

'Moon bought into the business.'

'Yeah. And one thing led to another. And they end up funding a movie that Buddy Bollen was making.'

'Which movie?' I said.

'Got me,' Eddie said.

'Did they fund more than one?' I said.

'Got me again,' Eddie said. 'I tole you what I know.'

'So you don't know if they're still connected?' I said.

'Nope.'

'You said before that no one ever didn't pay Moon. Why is that?'

'That people always paid?'

'Yes.'

Eddie turned and looked at me for the first time.

'Say it was you,' Eddie said. 'And you owed Moon and you didn't make your payment. Somebody would come and talk to you. Then you still don't pay, and somebody comes and slaps you around a little. Not bad, nothing broken, just get your attention. And you still don't pay and somebody comes by and, maybe, shoots your dog. Then they hurt your husband or your mother or your friend. No deaths, but hurt. They tell your husband or your mother or your friend why they're getting hurt. Maybe they'll cough up the dough. Maybe not. Puts a lot of pressure on you. Now and then they come by and hurt you, too, but not so bad that you can't pay up.'

'Would he ever kill me?'

'Not until he got his dough.'

'But he'd kill other people.'

'Sure,' Eddie said. 'Sooner or later. And once he got his dough from you.'

Eddie pretended to slit his throat with his forefinger.

'So I'd be better off not to pay.'

'Be a judgment you'd have to make,' Eddie said. 'Myself, I'd find the money.'

'What if I went away?' I said. 'Moved, left no address.'

'Moon would look for you for as long as it took. Anyone knew where you were, Moon would make them tell. If nobody knew, he'd keep looking. He's got some people don't do nothing else but skipchase.'

'You'd have to kill him,' Felix said.

'And most of his crew,' Eddie said. 'Hard to do.'

Felix made his peculiar laugh noise again. Rosie opened her obsidian eyes and looked at him.

'But not impossible,' Felix said.

Eddie shrugged and turned back to look at the donut shop.

I said, 'Rosie?' and held up her leash. She sat up and looked and scrambled over Felix's thick torso to the backseat. I hooked her leash on.

'You gonna run this down,' Felix said. 'I know that. You get involved with anything gonna annoy Moon Monaghan, and you let me know. You can't deal with him by yourself.'

'I'll be all right, Felix.'

'Not if you fuck with Moon Monaghan,' Felix said. 'You call me.'

Felix looked at me. I nodded.

I said 'Thank you' to the back of Eddie's head. He nodded, and Rosie and I got out of the car. Felix stayed where he was until I got in my car and drove away.

31

It took two days and several phone exchanges with an assistant named Veronique to finally get through to Tony Gault. When I finally did, it was six o'clock eastern time on a cold Monday. I was sitting at my kitchen counter with a glass of white wine when he called me back.

'Sorry, sorry, sorry,' he said when I answered. 'I got back to you as quickly as I could.'

'Which was as soon as there was no one more important to call,' I said.

'Of course,' Tony said. 'I'm a Hollywood agent.'

'You're fun despite that,' I said.

'We both are,' Tony said.

I drank some of my wine. 'What do you know about an organization called Hollywood Investment Team?'

Tony laughed. 'HIT,' he said.

'Hit?'

'The initials spell *hit*. That's why they called themselves that.'

'Oh,' I said, 'of course.'

'They arranged financing,' Tony said.

'Why the past tense?' I said.

'Company was run by two guys,' Tony said. 'Lawyer named Arlo Delaney, and a financial type named Greg Newton. I think he shortened it from Nootangian.'

'Clever name change,' I said.

'Isn't it?' Tony said. 'I don't know the details. But last summer somebody shot them. I don't know if the company actually exists anymore.'

'Arlo Delaney?' I said.

'Yeah. The lawyer.'

'Well, pretend they're alive,' I said. 'Tell me about the company.'

'Find a film project that's floundering,' Tony said. 'Put it together with an investor who wants to be a movie mogul.'

'What does the investor get out of it?'

'Depends,' Tony said, 'on how good his lawyer was when they made the deal. If he gets a percentage of the profits, he gets nothing. I know accountants who could prove that *Gone with the Wind* showed no profit.'

I drank some wine.

'What would be a good deal?' I said.

'Percent of the gross is nice, maybe some of the back end.'

'Back end?'

'Like foreign sales. Sometimes a guy will buy the rights to the foreign sales of a film before the film is made. The filmmaker takes the money, makes the film, makes money, he hopes, on domestic box office, and the investors get to sell the film abroad.'

'Can you do that with other rights?'

My glass was empty. I poured some more wine.

'Sure. Television. Video. Novelization – stuff like that,' Tony said.

'And if the foreign sales don't happen? Or whatever?'

'Then the investor is, as we shrewd financial manipulators say, fucked.'

'So there's risk,' I said.

'Sure. There's risk investing in the S&P 500,' Tony said.

'And does the investor always know the risk?'

'Of course not. It depends on who did the negotiating and what questions they asked,' Tony said. 'There are smart businessmen who want to be in the movie business so bad that they agree to nonsense, as long as someone will take their money.'

'What was HIT's reputation?' I said.

Tony laughed a little on his end of the phone.

'They didn't fund a lot of Oscar winners.'

'What did they fund?'

'Porn,' Tony said. 'Movies you see on cable starring people you never heard of. Some guy's pet movie project – he'll do anything to get it made, so it can show once in an art house in Des Moines.'

'Were they honest?'

'God no,' Tony said. 'Why should they be different?'

I had some wine.

'Corruption is everywhere,' I said.

'Thank God,' Tony said. 'It's what allows me to flourish.'

'Where were they killed?'

'I don't know.'

'Do you know where their office was?' I said.

'Hollywood, someplace, hold on a second…'

I heard him speak off the phone. 'Veronique, do we still have HIT in the Rolodex? … Delaney and Newton … yeah, that's it … write it down for me … thanks.'

He came back to me.

'Office was in Hollywood on Gower,' he said.

'Thank you,' I said.

'Is this part of the same case?' Tony said. 'Buddy Bollen and Erin Flint and all that?'

'Maybe,' I said.

'And that's all you're going to tell me,' Tony said.

'I don't know much more than that,' I said. 'Yet.'

'I like the *yet*,' Tony said. 'Confident.' He was quiet.

'Will this bring you back out here?' he said after a while.

'It might,' I said.

'I hope so.'

'Me too,' I said.

Again, quiet for a moment across the three-thousand-mile connection.

'Are you being faithful to me?' Tony said.

'Sadly, yes.'

'Because the opportunity hasn't presented itself?' Tony said.
'Sadly, yes.'
'So,' he said, 'maybe you better hurry on out here.'
'And, of course, you've been faithful?'
'I'm a Hollywood agent,' Tony said.
'I withdraw the question,' I said.
'But I remind you, again,' he said. 'I am fun.'
'What else is there?' I said.

32

I went to see my shrink. I didn't go regularly anymore, but I was always welcome when I needed an appointment. I was usually kind of glad to need an appointment. Being with her made me feel safe. She seemed always to know. Even when she didn't say much of anything, I always left feeling that I knew.

The nameplate on the front door was discreet: SUSAN SILVERMAN. Nothing else, no title before, no degrees after. I went in and sat in her waiting room, and looked at *The New Yorker,* and listened to the white-sound machine, not looking up when the preceding client left and Dr Silverman came to the waiting-room door and beckoned me in. She was wearing black slacks and a gray tweed jacket. Her thick, dark hair gleamed and her makeup was perfect and understated. I knew shrinks toned down when they were working. Even so, she was the most pulled-together woman I had ever seen. As always, I wondered what she looked like when she went out.

'Richie's wife is pregnant,' I said without preamble. 'A boy.'

'Oh?'

'Which means it's over,' I said.

'How so?' Dr Silverman said.

'I'm out of Richie's life,' I said. 'He'll have the son he always wanted. I know him. He won't change his mind.'

'Very little in life is certain,' Dr Silverman said.

'Are you suggesting I cling to the hope that he'll come back?'

'Is that what you've been doing?'

'I guess so.'

'And you feel that it's no longer appropriate?'

'Appropriate,' I said. 'Why do shrinks always say things like "appropriate?"'

'We try to be nonjudgmental,' Dr Silverman said.

'So something's appropriate or inappropriate?' I said. 'And that's not judgmental?'

'Behavior is consistent with the causative circumstance or it's not,' she said. 'It's an assessment of behavior, not a judgment of worth.'

'Oh, shit,' I said.

Dr Silverman cocked her head slightly but didn't say anything. She waited.

'I've met an interesting man,' I said.

She nodded.

'He's the chief of police in the town of Paradise.'

She nodded again.

'He's divorced but trying to reconcile.'

Nod.

'Do you think it's appropriate?' I said.

'Do you?' Dr Silverman said.

'I asked you first,' I said.

She smiled.

'What about it might be inappropriate?' Dr Silverman said.

'He's trying to reconcile with his ex-wife,' I said. 'I don't want to ruin that for him.'

'You feel he's drawn to you?'

'Yes.'

'And you're drawn to him?'

'Yes. I think so.'

Dr Silverman sat perfectly still. Her hands were motionless in her lap. She waited.

'So maybe he should be allowed to choose?' I said.

Dr Silverman smiled.

'All's … appropriate … in love and war?'

Dr Silverman raised her eyebrows slightly but didn't speak.

'Maybe I shouldn't be worried about her?' I said.

'Are you worried about her?'

'I … I don't even know her,' I said.

Dr Silverman nodded.

'So maybe I'm not worried about her,' I said.

Dr Silverman did something with her eyes that, I had learned, meant follow that thought.

'So what am I worried about?'

She smiled. I sat. She waited.

'Give me a hint,' I said.

'I don't know what you are worried about, but we both know what most people worry about.'

'Themselves,' I said.

She smiled. I sat. Neither of us spoke.

After a while, I said, 'I'm worried about myself. I'm scared that if I commit to Jesse, I'll let go of Richie.'

I don't know how she let me know. She didn't say anything. She didn't seem to do anything. But I knew she thought I was right.

33

'Cronjager got back to me last night,' Jesse said.

He and I were sitting near the window with a view of the harbor in a restaurant called the Gray Gull.

'And?' I said.

'Delaney and Newton were shot to death with the same nine-millimeter,' Jesse said. 'Delaney took four in the chest and one in the head. Newton took three in the chest, one in the head.'

'The one in the head was from close range?' I said.

'Yeah,' Jesse said. 'Pays to make sure. The office computer was missing. There were no files.'

'Was there any sign that there might have been files?'

'There was an empty two-drawer file cabinet,' Jesse said.

'So whoever shot them must have had reason to think he was in the files?'

Jesse nodded. The waitress came with menus. We asked for iced tea while we read the menu.

'What's good here?' I said.

'The view,' Jesse said.
'Oh,' I said.
The waitress brought the iced tea. We ordered. The waitress departed.
'Cronjager got tax returns from the IRS,' Jesse said. 'Nothing.'
'Buddy wasn't mentioned?'
'Nope.'
'Moon Monaghan?'
'Nope.'
'And of course no Erin Flint,' I said.
Jesse shook his head. 'These guys took a big net loss each of the last several years.'
'People lie on their tax returns,' I said.
'I've heard that.'
'But they have to keep their own records,' I said, 'or they won't know what they're doing.'
'Which is probably why the computer is missing and there's nothing in the file cabinet,' Jesse said.
The waitress brought us two chef salads and refilled our iced-tea glasses. The day was dark. The harbor water looked murky and cold. The boats in the harbor floated silent and sparse at their moorings. Across the harbor I could see Paradise Neck, and half closing the harbor mouth I could see Stiles Island, where Buddy Bollen lived in style.
'Well,' I said. 'If my sources are correct, two of the principals are here in Boston, available for conversation.'
'They probably will not confess,' Jesse said.
'But if we pry away at them,' I said, 'something might pry loose and then ... who knows?'
'Maybe he'll do something stupid,' Jesse said, 'and we can catch him doing it.'
'We can try,' I said.
'Who you want to start with,' Jesse said.
'Monaghan.'
'Fine,' Jesse said. 'You know where he is?'
'Uncle Felix will know,' I said.
Jesse smiled at me.
'You have got the damnedest set of connections, Sunny. Your

father's a cop and your uncle's a crook.'

'Actually, my ex-husband's uncle. But he likes me.'

'Who wouldn't,' Jesse said.

'Felix says Monaghan is very dangerous.'

'We'll talk with him together,' Jesse said.

'Felix said I should let him know if I'm going to, ah, "fuck with Moon Monaghan."'

'So to speak,' Jesse said.

'Metaphorically,' I said.

'We're pretty dangerous, too,' Jesse said.

'And Felix?' I said.

'Up to you, he's your ex-uncle-in-law,' Jesse said.

'Perhaps we'll hold him in reserve,' I said.

We were quiet for a time, concentrating on our mediocre chef salads. When I had enough, I put my fork down and blotted my lips with my napkin, and took out my lip gloss.

'I hope you don't mind,' I said.

'I like it,' Jesse said. 'I'll take all the womanliness I can get.'

I finished with my lip gloss and looked at him.

'How are you?' I said.

'Lousy,' Jesse said.

'Your ex-wife?' I said.

'Yes.'

I was quiet. I decided to let it sit. He'd talk when he was ready. I would, too.

'Well,' I said after a time, 'you're still drinking iced tea at lunch.'

'So far,' Jesse said.

34

When Felix called me with Moon Monaghan's address in Chestnut Hill, he said, 'That cop you're going to see Moon with – he any good?'

'Yes,' I said. 'I think he is.'

'Small-town cop?'

'Used to be a homicide detective in Los Angeles,' I said.

'Cops don't scare Moon much,' Felix said.
'Do you?'
'Not enough,' Felix said.
'We'll have a couple of state troopers with us,' I said to Felix, 'giving us jurisdiction, sort of.'
'Good,' Felix said. 'I'll let Moon know you're with me.'
'Don't warn him we're coming,' I said.
Felix made his laugh noise again.
'I'll just let him know, like generally, that you're with me and Desmond.'
'Thank you, Felix.'
'Be careful of Moon,' Felix said. 'I don't even scare him very much.'
'You're too modest,' I said.
'Just be careful,' Felix said.
And we hung up.

Moon Monaghan lived in a big brick house with a view of the reservoir. I went with Jesse in a Paradise police cruiser, which Jesse drove.
A state police cruiser followed us. Moon's house was close to the road, with a short, wide driveway leading to a two-car garage. Jesse parked in the driveway, next to a BMW sportscar. The state police cruiser U-turned and parked on the street in front of Moon's house.
'What did you tell him?' I said.
'Moon? I didn't talk with Moon. I talked with his lawyer. I said we needed to talk with Moon about a crime we were investigating. I said we had no evidence that he was involved but that we hoped he could clear up some things for us. And I said, out of respect, we would come to him and not ask him to come out to Paradise and sit in the interrogation room.'
'Do you actually have an interrogation room?' I said.
'No.'
A housekeeper let us in and led us to the living room. Moon was there with his lawyer. The lawyer was bulky and red-faced with a lot of silver-gray hair brushed straight back. He had on a double-breasted gray glen plaid suit, a red tie, and a blue shirt with a white

collar. He had a briefcase with him, so we'd know he was a lawyer. Moon was something else again. He was very tall, maybe 6'5' or 6'6'. He was angular with big hands, long fingers, and prominent knuckles. His skin was very pale, as if he never went out. His hair was long and white-blond and combed back smooth and tight against his long skull. The lawyer rose when we came in. Moon didn't.

'I'm Francis Clough,' he said. 'I represent Mr. Monaghan.'

'Jesse Stone,' Jesse said. 'Sunny Randall.'

Moon looked at us with eyes so pale it was hard to tell they were blue.

'Please sit down,' Clough said.

Jesse ignored him.

''Mind if I call you Moon?' he said.

'I don't give a fuck what you call me,' Moon said.

His voice was flat and whispery, with no inflection, as if he had a mechanical throat.

'So, Moon,' Jesse said. 'Have you ever been involved in the movie business?'

'No.'

'Ever invest in any movie projects?'

'No.'

'Do you know a man named Buddy Bollen?'

'No.'

'Moon, Moon,' Jesse said. 'We have pretty good information that you invested in a film project with Buddy Bollen.'

'Yeah?'

Jesse nodded.

'Prove it,' Moon said.

'If you have any allegations against my client ...' Clough said.

'Francis,' Moon said. 'I talk. You listen. You hear one of my rights being violated, speak up. Otherwise, shut the fuck up.'

'Sure, Moon.'

'You got anything else to ask me?' Moon said.

'Do you know anyone named Arlo Delaney?' Jesse said.

He stood in front of Moon as he spoke, and looked down at him. I stood in the open doorway and leaned on the jamb.

'No.'

'Moon,' I said from the doorway. 'He's your cousin.'

'Never heard of him.'

'And a fella named Newton, Greg Newton?' Jesse said.

'Probably shortened from Nootangian,' I said.

'Don't know him,' Moon said.

'Do you know what time it is?' Jesse said.

'No.'

'Nice to find consistency,' Jesse said. 'What do you do for a living?'

'I'm retired.'

'From what?' I said.

'Nothing.'

'And for income?' I said.

Moon almost smiled.

'Social security,' he said. 'Plus, I got an IRA, couple mutual funds.'

'Waste not, want not,' I said.

'And I know about you, too, little girl,' Moon said. 'I know you're with the Burkes. Just don't think it buys you anything with me.'

'You have nothing I'd want to buy,' I said.

He stared at me. Jesse moved slightly to his left and met Moon's stare as if he were intercepting it. Neither blinked for a time.

Then Moon said, 'And being the fucking police chief in some hick fucking town don't buy much from me, either.'

Jesse kept his gaze on Moon for a little bit longer, then he smiled.

'Damn,' Jesse said. 'I was hoping it would.'

35

I worked out with Erin Flint in the private gym at SeaChase where Misty had died. Erin was wearing a cropped black tank top and shorts. I had on sweatpants and a loose gray T-shirt. Working out with Erin was not a good time to be showing off my body. Two security guards stood at the far end of the gym on either side of the door.

'Do you know a man named Moon Monaghan?' I said.

'Moon? Sure. He produced my first picture, him and Buddy.'

'Really?' I said. 'Very tall? Phony-looking platinum-blond hair?'

'Yeah. He used to date Misty.'

'She like him?'

'No. She thought he was creepy.'

'Why did she go out with him?'

'Buddy made her,' Erin said.

'How?' I said.

'How did he make her?'

I nodded.

'He just did. He told her Moon was important to the project.'

Erin was doing one of those hideous butt exercises where you are on all fours and push up a weight backward with one leg, then the other. She paused and looked up at me from her hands and knees.

'Besides, we used to be whores,' she said. 'It wasn't that big a deal.'

I nodded. She remained on her hands and knees.

'Actually,' she said after a moment, 'I fucked him a couple of times, too.'

'How was that?' I said.

The thought of it was chilling, and I didn't really want to know how it was. But I wanted to keep on the topic of Moon Monaghan, and I couldn't think of anything else.

'Like a trip to the gyno,' Erin said.

'Clinical?' I said.

'Yeah, that's a good word,' Erin said. 'He was clinical.'

'And you had sex with him because he was important to the project?'

'Of course,' Erin said.

She began another set of butt shapers. It seemed effortless, and she showed no sign of strain.

'Certainly not for fun,' she said.

'Who do you sleep with for fun?' I said. 'Buddy?'

I didn't know where I was going, but it was better than going nowhere.

'Buddy? Do you think it would be fun to fuck Buddy?'

'Can't say that I do,' I said. 'So who's fun?'

She came out of her hands-and-knees stance and sat on the

floor with her back against one of the exercise machines and her amazing legs spraddled out in front of her.

'Who do I fuck for fun?'

I nodded.

'And what makes that your business?'

'I'm detecting,' I said.

She sat on the floor and thought about it.

'You know,' she said after a while, 'I can't think of anybody. How 'bout you?'

'They've all been fun,' I said.

'All?'

'Not actually that many,' I said. 'I was married for a while.'

'But not now,' Erin said.

'No.'

'Now you're just giving it away when you can.'

I was having an actual conversation with Erin. I hated to lose it. On the other hand, I didn't feel like explaining my sex life to her.

'I have met some men I liked,' I said. 'We have had some fun. Part of the fun is sex. But it's not the only part.'

'Isn't that ... cute?' Erin said.

'It's never been fun for you?' I said.

'Honey,' she said. 'I been a working girl since my mother died.'

Sitting on the floor with her legs splayed, she opened her arms wide.

'And this,' she said, 'is what I've got to work with.'

I smiled at her. 'Well, it's a wonderful instrument,' I said.

'Yeah,' she said. 'It is.'

'Does Moon Monaghan know much about producing pictures?' I said.

'God no,' Erin said. 'He's just a money guy.'

She laughed.

'Wants to be in show business,' she said. 'When we were shooting *Woman Warrior,* the first one, he was on the set every day, hanging around, trying to score any actress he could get near. Drove Buddy crazy. Drove everybody crazy. In the way. Stupid. He was like a fucking tourist.'

'So he invested in the show?'

'Yeah. And insisted on a producing credit,' Erin said.

'Do you know how much he put in?'
She shrugged.
'Nope,' she said. 'You'll have to ask Buddy.'
'But that was why he was important,' I said. 'Money.'
'Yep.'
She stood and arched her back a bit to stretch it, and walked toward the gravitron machine. She laughed without any amusement.
'The Boverini sisters,' she said. 'Right back where we started, fucking for money.'
'And Buddy got the money?' I said.
'Naturally,' Erin said.
'So, to extend the analogy,' I said, 'Buddy would be the pimp?'
'I don't know what an analogy is,' Erin said. 'But Buddy would make a good pimp.'
'Better than Gerard?'
'Gerard,' she said. 'Compared to Buddy, Gerard was … ah … what? … human … you know? … he was like a person. Buddy's a windup piggy bank.'
'Do you see Moon Monaghan anymore?' I said.
'No, not since a little after the first picture.'
'*Woman Warrior*?' I said.
'Yes. He financed the first *Woman Warrior* picture, and used to come around after, for a while, bang one of the Boverini girls, or both of them. He liked a doubleheader now and then. Then he stopped showing up. Buddy never said anything about him.'
'Did *Woman Warrior* make money?'
'Sure. It was a big hit.'
'You know how much it made?'
'No, I just know Buddy said it did really well.'
'Have you heard from Gerard since you went with Buddy?'
'He sent me flowers the day after *Woman Warrior* opened.'
'All right, Gerard,' I said. 'So he knew how to find you.'
'He knew I was with Buddy,' she said. 'Why you asking me all this stuff?'
'Investigating,' I said. 'You never know what information will be useful.'
'Here's some information,' Erin said. 'They don't want me to

play ball and they killed my sister by mistake.'

'Is that why there's so much security?' I said. 'Because of you?'

'Well, my God,' Erin said. 'They killed my sister.'

'I mean before that. I understand that you're a star and he's famous for his wealth. But the amount of security at his house and everywhere even before Misty was killed … I just wondered?'

Erin shrugged her shoulders and stepped up onto the gravitron and began to do dips.

She said, 'I'm a damned movie star, you know.'

'Did the security increase after *Woman Warrior*?'

'I don't know. I guess so. There were a couple guys around. Buddy's driver. Couple guys at the house.'

'But after *Woman Warrior*?'

'More guys came aboard,' she said.

'Fame has its price,' I said.

'Wait'll I play in the big leagues this summer,' she said.

'You're not scared?' I said.

'Fuck them,' Erin said, 'I'm going to do it. I'm going to do it.'

'Them?'

'All of them,' she said.

'Men?' I said.

'Every fucking one of them,' she said.

36

'Tony Gault told me,' I said to Jesse, 'that if you sign onto a movie deal and don't know much, you could end up with a percentage of the profit.'

'Uh-huh.'

Jesse had put a bowl of water on his office floor for Rosie, and she was drinking from it and making a lot of noise.

'And he told me that there were accountants out there who could make it look like *Gone with the Wind* didn't make a profit.'

'Which is why you're better off,' Jesse said, 'with a piece of the gross.'

'I forgot for a moment that you used to live out there,' I said.

'And my wife was an actress – sort of.'

'I forgot that, too,' I said. 'So you know all this?'

'Everybody in LA knows all this,' Jesse said.

Rosie continued to slurp at the water dish.

'But maybe if you were a shylock from Boston,' I said, 'and you trusted your cousin, you might not know all this.'

'Especially if you were a dumb shylock,' Jesse said.

'You think Moon is dumb?'

'Moon's success is rooted in greed and meanness,' Jesse said. 'Got nothing to do with smart.'

'So, say this dumb shylock puts a bunch of cash into a movie. He has a bunch of cash, thinks putting it into the movie will launder it. He gets a nice piece of the profit. And he gets to hang around with movie stars.'

'Heaven,' Jesse said. 'You think your dog is going to stop drinking anytime soon?'

'She takes tiny, ladylike swallows,' I said. 'So she has to do it for a while.'

Jesse nodded. Rosie continued to slurp.

'So,' Jesse said. 'Suppose Moon puts a lot of money into this *Woman Warrior* movie. Do you know how it did?'

'It may not even matter with creative accounting,' I said. 'It could have tanked for real, or Buddy could have cheated him.'

'Our Buddy?' Jesse said.

'Just supposing,' I said. 'Either way, Moon's out his original investment and any earnings he might have hoped for.'

'Which no one likes,' Jesse said. 'But shylocks hate.'

'Hate,' I said.

'And if we believe Uncle Felix's guy, Eddie,' Jesse said, 'Moon's collection technique is to spare the debtor and kill people around him.'

'And according to Erin, he'd been to the house and knew the sister,' I said.

Rosie stopped drinking water. Jesse looked down at her.

'Already?' he said.

'Rosie believes in moderation,' I said.

Rosie came around Jesse's desk and lay down on her side on the floor under my chair with her feet out straight. Her small body was so muscular that the top set of feet stuck straight out in the air.

'This line of thinking gives us a nice suspect,' Jesse said.

'Our first one,' I said.

'Well, I kind of liked the black-belt pimp from LA, too,' Jesse said.

'We can keep him in reserve,' I said.

'Bench strength,' Jesse said, 'is good.'

'Of course, we have absolutely no proof for anybody,' I said.

Jesse nodded. 'And if it turns out that *Woman Warrior* turned a profit, might shake our theory a little,' he said.

'I wonder if we can get an audit,' I said.

'Probable cause?' Jesse said.

'None,' I said.

Jesse didn't say anything.

'I can ask Tony Gault what he knows, and what he can find out.'

Jesse nodded. He appeared to be looking thoughtfully at Rosie.

'You like Chinese food?' Jesse said.

'I do.'

'Would you care to come to my place tonight,' Jesse said, 'and eat some with me?'

'Why yes I would,' I said.

37

Jesse Stone's condo was on the harborfront, with a small balcony off the living room that jutted out over the water. Framed on the wall behind the bar in the living room was a huge black-and-white photograph of a baseball player diving sideways, reaching for the ball.

'Who's that?' I said.

'Ozzie Smith.'

'I knew it wasn't you,' I said.

'Because he's wearing a big-league unie?'

'Well, that,' I said. 'And he's black.'

'Oh, yeah.'

'Why is he there?'

'Best shortstop I ever saw,' Jesse said. 'If I made a martini, would you drink it?'

'Up, with olives,' I said.

He went to the bar and made a shaker of martinis and poured two. Mine with olives, his over ice with a twist.

'Can I have a tour?' I said.

'Won't take long,' Jesse said.

There was a kitchen, a bedroom, a bath off the bedroom, and the living/dining area with the bar. The place was very neat. On the night table by the bed was a photograph of a good-looking woman.

'Is that your ex-wife?' I said.

'Yes,' Jesse said.

We walked back into the living room.

'In good weather it's nice to have a drink outside, on the little balcony,' Jesse said.

'Unless you're not drinking,' I said.

Jesse took a small sip of his martini and smiled at me over the rim of the glass.

'Or you are trying to drink socially,' he said, 'like a responsible adult.'

'How's that going?' I said.

Jesse lowered the glass and his smile got wider.

'This is my first night,' he said.

I looked out through the French doors at the harbor, and the lights across.

'You like it here?' I said.

Jesse came and stood beside me. He was quiet for a moment.

Then he said, 'Yes. I guess I do.'

'Different than Los Angeles,' I said.

'Yes.'

'You can make a difference here,' I said.

'Yes.'

We stood quietly, holding our martinis, looking at the harbor.

'In LA,' Jesse said, 'any big city, you're just bailing a leaky boat. You don't sink, but you can't stop bailing, you know?'

'Too much crime,' I said.

'Here there's not so much,' Jesse said. 'You have a significant crime, here, you solve it, you restore the whole town.'

'So the town becomes yours,' I said. 'In a way that LA never could be.'

'Yes.'

We each drank a bit of martini. There was enough moonlight so we could see the water. It was cold and uninviting, but there was something eternal about it.

'You get the constituency small enough,' I said, 'and it can become yours.'

'Why you quit the cops?' Jesse said.

'I suppose so. That and the, ah, chain of command.'

'Ah, yes,' Jesse said.

My glass was empty. Jesse took it and went to the bar and made me another martini. His glass was half full. Though, with a lot of ice in there, it was a little hard to tell. He brought my glass back to me and we stood and looked at the harbor some more.

'So you're home,' I said.

Jesse thought about it.

'It's what I have,' he said after a while. 'I struggle with booze. My love life is a mess. Being the Chief of Police in Paradise, Massachusetts, is what I've got.'

'Love life is not the same as sex life,' I said.

'No,' he said. 'It isn't.'

I walked to the couch and sat at one end. Jesse turned, still by the balcony door, and looked at me.

'And sex life is an insufficient substitute,' I said.

'It is,' Jesse said. 'But better than no substitute.'

Jesse walked to a chair opposite the couch and sat. He drank a little more of his martini. I could feel his carefulness.

'Jenn is cheating again,' he said.

I felt as if I were watching a genie materialize out of a bottle. I nodded and didn't say anything.

'I guess it's time to talk about it,' Jesse said.

He got up and made himself a second drink and sat back down in his chair.

'Ever since I was with her, Jenn had a tendency to wander. At first I didn't know it. Then I did, and figured there was something wrong with me. I drank too much. I was just a cop. I expected her to feel about me the way I felt about her. I held on to her too hard. Stuff like that.'

'If it was your fault, you could fix it,' I said.

'You've been shrunk, too,' he said. 'And there was stuff wrong with me, and I did work on it. I still work on it.'

He paused and drank.

'In fact, I see a guy that Jenn found, got me to go to, when I first got here.'

'She was here?' I said.

'She came here.'

'From Los Angeles?' I said.

Jesse nodded.

'Got a job as a weather girl,' he said. 'Channel three.'

'Jenn Stone,' I said. 'That's where I've seen her.'

'That's her with the low-pressure areas,' Jesse said, 'and the occluded fronts waving at the weather charts just like she knew.'

'She followed you here?' I said.

'Yeah.'

'So there's a real connection between you?'

'Especially when things are going badly for her.'

'It's an impulse I understand,' I said.

'She's done a lot of shrink work, too,' Jesse said.

'But not enough?'

Jesse shrugged.

'She was here last year doing a TV special on Race Week,' he said, 'and she stayed with me. It went well. I thought both of us had turned a corner.'

He looked at his glass but didn't drink. He looked at mine. I had some left.

'When the special was through shooting, she went back to her place in Boston,' Jesse said. 'We agreed we could be together without living together. Our only rule was monogamy.'

He was silent. I sipped my drink and waited. He looked at his drink again, and again didn't drink any.

'She only sleeps with people who can help her: producers, casting agents, station managers, news directors.'

I nodded. Whatever else Jenn was, she was a powerful presence. I could feel her in the room.

'This time she's fucking the new station manager,' Jesse said.

His voice was harsh. His choice of the ugliest verb, I knew, was deliberate. I'd made the same choice several times. I wanted to ask him how he knew, or if he was sure. I didn't. I knew how irrelevant and maybe embarrassing questions like that were.

'Last straw?' I said.

He nodded slowly.

'It's over,' he said.

I nodded. There was nothing to say. He finished his drink in a swallow. He stared at the empty glass for a moment, then put it on the coffee table. I drank the remainder of mine.

'Make you another?' he said.

'No,' I said. 'Not right now. Maybe wine with dinner.'

He nodded and smiled at me. It was a real smile, though not awfully happy.

'Okay,' he said. 'I showed you mine. You want to show me yours?'

'It seems only fair,' I said.

38

I talked about Richie. About the marriage, and the divorce, and his remarriage.

'And now his new wife is pregnant,' I said.

Jesse nodded.

'Over?' he said.

'Over.'

We both sat for a time with our glasses empty and no sound in the room.

'So we're both feeling pretty bad right now,' Jesse said.

'And we're pretty desperately in need of consolation,' I said.

'And would be inclined to make a casual something into more than it was.'

'We both know that,' I said.

'On the other hand,' Jesse said. 'There's nothing wrong with consolation.'

'Or revenge,' I said.

Jesse smiled. I smiled. We sat still for a moment and looked at each other.

'Do you think we should be careful?' I said.

'I think we should have sex,' Jesse said.

'But carefully,' I said.

'Let's agree beforehand,' he said. 'Not to marry right away.'

'Okay,' I said.

He stood. I stood. We looked at each other for a moment. Then we put our arms round each other. We kissed each other. I could feel it starting. *Here we go,* I thought.

'Do you need to sit on the couch,' Jesse said, 'and have kissyface foreplay first?'

'No,' I said.

'Good.'

We walked together to his bedroom.

'Do you prefer under the covers?' Jesse said.

'No,' I said, 'restrictive.'

He nodded and began to unbutton his shirt. I began to undress with him. I had given it such thought when I'd dressed. Maybe I was expecting sex, maybe I wasn't. I dropped my shirt on the floor. I didn't want to show up in thong underpants, a frilly skirt, and fuck-me shoes, carrying a sign that said, *I'm here to bop your brains out!* On the other hand, I didn't want to look like somebody's maiden aunt with white cotton panties and Hush Puppies. My high boots, with no side zipper, looked great. But they were nearly impossible to get off. So were my front-button jeans. I opted for a skirt. It would be easy to remove, and, if it came to that, he could help me with the boots. It had come to that. I sat on the bed in my bra and skirt.

'Jesse,' I said. 'You'll have to help me with the boots.'

He was down to his shorts, black watch boxers. He wasn't terribly big, but every muscle in his torso was defined. Each abdominal muscle was distinct. He smiled at me.

'Plan ahead,' he said.

'I was ambivalent,' I said.

He took hold of one boot and I leaned back on the bed and we wrestled it off. When we got the other one off, Jesse ran his hand along my calf.

'On the other hand,' he said, 'you shaved your legs.'

'I said I was ambivalent.'

Jesse lined my boots up neatly in front of his bedroom chair. His back was as muscular as his front, and, thank God, not hairy.

I stood and unzipped my skirt and let it drop to the floor.

'Black undies?' he said. 'How ambivalent were you?'

'Black, yes, cut high, yes,' I said. 'But no ribbons, no lace, no bows, no see-through.'

'Prim,' Jesse said.

I unsnapped my bra and shrugged out of it, letting it slide down my arms.

'The dead giveaway,' I said, 'was the shaved legs. I spent some time thinking about it. If I shaved them, was I committing ahead of time to sex?'

'And you shaved them.'

'Uh-huh.'

'That's key,' Jesse said.

'Uh-huh.'

I slipped my thumbs inside the waistband of my middle-of-the-road black panties, and slipped them off, and stepped out of them. Jesse took off his shorts. We looked for a moment at each other, and then, in some kind of mutual moment, we both jumped on the bed together, giggling. We put our arms around each other, and, pressed tight together, we began to kiss. We kissed for a while. We explored a bit. Then Jesse paused and rolled onto his back.

'What?' I said.

'A symbolic thing,' he said.

He reached over to his night table and took the picture of Jenn and turned it facedown.

'Over,' he said.

And rolled back toward me.

'Was it the leg shave?' I murmured.

'Probably,' Jesse said.

And then neither of us said anything coherent for quite a long time.

39

We lay naked together getting our breathing under control. The bedclothes had long since been discarded and were somewhere tangled on the floor with my clothes. My head was on Jesse's shoulder. Both of us felt a little damp. Our breathing slowed. It was as if I had been a long way and was slowly returning.

'Agile,' Jesse said.

'Vigorous,' I said.

We both smiled and lay quietly, taking in air.

'Not since I first married Jenn …' Jesse said.

'Have you had sex like this,' I said.

'Yes,' he said.

'Is that something you say to all the girls?'

'It is,' Jesse said. 'But this time I mean it.'

'I know,' I said.

The stillness in Jesse's condo was soothing. The faint smell of the ocean was clean and pleasant. I rubbed my forehead against his jaw.

'You shaved, too,' I said.

'Ever hopeful,' he said.

'And,' I said, 'the bed is freshly made.'

'It's good to be ready,' he said.

The room was bright. We had not bothered to turn out the lights. Jesse's breathing was easy now. So was mine.

'Did you ever hear of a story called *A Clean, Well-Lighted Place*?' I said.

'No.'

'I read it in college,' I said. 'I didn't get it then. Now I do.'

'Is it about sex?' Jesse said.

'No,' I said. 'More about peace, maybe, or refuge.'

Jesse didn't say anything for a while. Neither did I.

Then Jesse said, 'This is pretty peaceful.'

'Yes,' I said.

Jesse's left arm was under my shoulders. His right hand rested on my stomach. Faintly, in the kitchen, I could hear the refrigerator cycle on. Somewhere outside, a car door closed. I continued to rub my forehead softly against his jaw.

'Everything seems to go back to Los Angeles,' Jesse said.

'Excuse me?'

'The case,' Jesse said. 'Misty's murder. All the connections seem to connect back to LA.'

I laughed to myself. Jesse felt the silent laughter.

'Insufficiently romantic?' Jesse said.

'The downside of sleeping with a cop, I guess.'

'It has its upside,' Jesse said. 'So to speak.'

'And thank God for it,' I said.

We both laughed.

'But think about it,' Jesse said. 'Erin and Misty are from LA. Buddy's from LA. They are connected to Moon Monaghan through an LA film financial outfit.'

'Erin's former pimp is still in LA,' I said.

'Erin and Misty's former pimp,' Jesse said.

'So he's connected to them,' I said. 'And they're connected to Buddy and he's connected to Moon, and Moon's connected to Delaney and Newton.'

'And …' Jesse said.

'And the chain stops,' I said. 'As far as we know.'

'Maybe we should know more,' I said.

'Can't hurt,' Jesse said.

He moved his hand gently down my stomach.

'You work through … Cronjager,' I said. 'I'll … work … through Erin.'

'See if we meet somewhere,' Jesse said.

His hand continued to move.

'Do we have an … ah … upside … again?' I said.

'I believe so,' Jesse said.

'Good for you,' I said.

We didn't get to the Chinese food until very late. Jesse reheated it in the oven, and we ate it for breakfast at his dining-room table, and watched the sun come slowly up over Paradise Neck, across the harbor.

40

Rosie and I sat in Spike's restaurant at a table near the door. There were no dogs allowed, but Rosie had a special relationship with the owner. It was the drink-after-work crowd, and the bar was busy. Spike was behind the bar, lending a hand. I ordered a Diet Coke and looked at the menu. If your taste ran to the ordinary, Spike put out a decent meal. Rosie sat in the chair beside me and waited patiently for the dog biscuit that she knew someone would bring her.

A squat man with a shaved head and a big mustache came into the restaurant wearing a gray warm-up jacket with red sleeves. He brushed by the hostess and sat down at my table. The word *Hurricanes* was stitched in red script across the front of the jacket. His hands were thick and he had the look of a bodybuilder. Rosie looked hard at him to see if he had a dog biscuit. He ignored her.

'You're Sunny Randall,' he said.

'Yes,' I said. 'This is Rosie.'

'Fuck Rosie,' he said. 'Moon wants to know why you're nosing around him.'

'We explained that not long ago to Moon himself,' I said.

'You and that cop.'

'Yes.'

'Maybe we can't do nothing about the cop,' the bald man said, 'but we can sure do something about you. Why you asking Moon a bunch of questions?'

'I'm flirtatious,' I said. 'And Moon is so cute.'

'Don't fuck with me,' the bald man said. 'I'll drag you outta here right now and beat the shit out of you.'

'You think?' I said.

He reached across the table and grabbed my face with one hand and squeezed. I knew that from behind the bar, Spike had seen him.

'I'd like it,' he said. 'I can make you squeal like a pig. Be fun.'

He gave me a little shake and let go. Spike came around the bar.

'So you can tell me now, nice and calm, or you can tell me

squealing and crying and blubbering for me to stop,' the bald man said.

I smiled. I think he felt Spike's looming appearance before he actually saw Spike. He may have been struck by how big Spike was, but Baldy was a professional tough guy. He stuck to his guns.

'Who the fuck are you?' he said.

'My name's Spike.'

'Well get lost, Spike. I'm talking to this lady.'

Spike looked at me.

'Get lost, Spike?' he said to me.

I smiled and nodded.

'Is he as annoying as he seems?' Spike said.

'Don't fuck with me, pal,' Baldy said. 'You don't know what you're getting into.'

Spike kept looking at him. The bald man stood suddenly and put his hand on Spike's chest and shoved. Nothing happened. Spike didn't move.

'Okay, pal,' Baldy said, 'it's your choice.'

He swung at Spike with a left hook. Spike caught it almost casually on his right forearm. He took hold of the man's shirt front with his left hand and yanked him off balance. He put his right hand into the bald man's crotch and picked him up bodily and raised him about chest level and slammed him flat on his back on the floor. It hadn't seemed that Spike was moving fast. But the whole thing took maybe a second. The bald man lay stunned. Spike put his foot on the bald man's neck.

'You got a gun?' Spike said.

The man was not out, but his brain was scrambled. He just stared up at Spike.

'If you got a gun,' Spike said, 'go for it, so I can break your neck.'

The bald man spread his hands as if to say *no, no.* Spike bent over and patted him down and took a short semiautomatic pistol from under his warm-up jacket. Spike stuck it in his hip pocket, then reached down and dragged Baldy to a semi-sitting position.

'If you bother her again,' Spike said softly, 'I will break your back and throw you in the harbor.'

The bald man nodded floppily, as if his coordination wasn't very good. Spike got him all the way to his feet. The restaurant was completely silent. Spike walked the man to the door and opened it and they both went outside. Spike was out there for maybe two minutes. Then he came back in. Under the table, I put my gun back in my purse.

'Drinks on the house,' Spike said to the bartenders, 'next round, everybody.'

Then he came and sat with me at the table.

'I put him in a cab,' Spike said.

Rosie looked at him to see if he had the dog biscuit. He didn't, but he saw the look and gestured at a waitress. She came with the biscuit and gave it to Rosie.

'So tell me about him,' Spike said.

41

The waitress came while I was talking. Spike looked at my empty glass.

'You want another drink?' Spike said.

'Diet Coke,' I said.

Spike raised his eyebrows.

'Jack Daniel's on the rocks,' Spike said. 'And a Diet Coke.'

Then he listened silently while I told him most of the rest of my story.

'So you think there might be some connection between this pimp,' Spike said, 'what's his name … ?'

'Gerard,' I said.

'Between Gerard and Moon?'

'When I can,' I said, 'I try not to think what is and what isn't before I know. It's just a possibility to look into.'

The waitress brought our drinks, and another cookie for Rosie.

'After this one,' I said, 'no more cookies for Rosie. I don't want her to get fat.'

'Nothing wrong with fat,' Spike said.

'You're not fat,' I said.

Spike smiled.

'I just look fat,' Spike said. 'Like Rosie.'

'She does not look fat,' I said. 'Neither one of you does.'

'In fact, we're built pretty much the same.'

'The scale is different,' I said.

Spike grinned. Rosie finished her cookie and lapped a crumb up off the tabletop.

'You think Moon is the one?' Spike said.

'If it were a guessing game,' I said, 'he'd be the best guess. But there's no real evidence against him.'

'So you're looking for a way in?' Spike said.

'Yes. Moon simply denies everything, and we have no leverage to make him do otherwise.'

I sipped my Diet Coke. Spike watched me.

'*We* would be you and the police chief up there,' Spike said.

'Yes,' I said.

He nodded and looked at my Diet Coke.

'Like that stuff?' he said.

'Not very much,' I said. 'But I thought I was drinking too much lately.'

Spike nodded.

'Does that mean you thought I was?' I said.

'Yeah.'

'Well, I've decided to cut back.'

'Starting now?' Spike said.

'Starting a couple of days ago, I guess.'

'What happened a couple of days ago?' Spike said.

I drank some Diet Coke. 'None of your business,' I said.

Spike took a sip of his drink and looked at the glass for a time.

'You get along with that police chief?' he said.

'Don't be so nosy,' I said.

'I heard he used to have a drinking problem,' Spike said.

'He did, but he's got it under control now,' I said.

'You too,' Spike said.

Rosie watched him closely. Experience had taught her that Spike was an excellent cookie source.

'I don't think I really had a problem,' I said. 'But things were piling up…'

'And now they aren't?' Spike said.

'I ...'

'Yes?'

'Are you suggesting that Jesse Stone and I have some sort of relationship?'

'Yes.'

'You son of a bitch,' I said.

'I'll take that as a yes?'

'How did you know?'

'I'm a sensitive gay man,' Spike said.

'You didn't seem so sensitive a while ago with that bald man.'

'I have my dark side,' Spike said.

'What if he comes back,' I said, 'looking for you, for revenge?'

'I'll kill him,' Spike said.

We were silent for a moment. We both knew that Spike meant it.

'Let me withdraw the question,' I said.

The restaurant was almost full by now. Many regulars recognized Rosie; a couple waved at her. An occasional person saw her sitting there and smiled and nudged a companion. Now and then someone looked askance. But no one complained. There was something about Spike that discouraged askance.

'So,' Spike said, 'you and the chief had sex yet?'

'God, you are sensitive,' I said.

'And it worked out well?'

'Yes.'

'And you're celebrating with a Diet Coke?' Spike said.

I smiled. 'It worked out well enough so I don't feel the need for anodynes.'

'Ano-what?'

'Pain relievers,' I said. 'You know what *anodyne* means as well as I do.'

Spike leaned across the table with his hand up, palm facing me. I slapped it.

'I like Richie,' Spike said.

'Me too.'

'But it is in your best interest to move on.'

'Day at a time,' I said.

'Day at a time,' Spike said.

42

Jesse came to my loft in the evening with a bottle of Iron Horse champagne. I put it in an ice bucket to chill while I gave him a tour. Touring my loft is not a long affair, even if you stop, as we did, to look at the half-done painting on the easel under my skylight.

'Park Street subway entrance,' Jesse said.

'Yes.'

'When it's done,' Jesse said, 'I'll like it.'

'You're interested in art?'

'No,' Jesse said. 'I'm interested in you.'

I nodded.

'That would be the better choice,' I said.

Lying on her side on my bed, Rosie watched us as we walked around. She had wagged her tail when she saw Jesse, but she was too deeply into lying on her side to get up and greet him. When the tour was over, I put out two champagne flutes, some cheese and fruit, and a loaf of French bread. Jesse opened the champagne and filled the glasses. We sat at my little table by the window. The cheese and bread did what Jesse couldn't. It stirred Rosie from the bed, and brought her to us.

'May I give her something?' Jesse said.

'She'll eat a grape,' I said.

Jesse pulled one from the cluster, put it in the palm of his hand, and handed it to Rosie. She took it happily, chewed it carefully, and swallowed.

'Lot of dogs don't like grapes,' Jesse said.

'Rosie is not like other dogs,' I said.

'Of course she's not,' Jesse said.

We clinked champagne glasses and drank.

'So,' I said. 'Is this business or pleasure?'

'I have a little information,' Jesse said, 'that Cronjager dug up for me.'

'So it's business,' I said.

'You are always a pleasure, Sunny.'

I nodded and took a small piece of cheese and ate it.

'So is it both?' I said.

'That would be something for both of us to say.'

I nodded again.

'When I knew you were coming over,' I said, 'my plan was to observe you closely, assess whether you were thinking we made a mistake the other night, see if you were feeling that maybe it was too much too fast, and never let on that I was worried about such matters. But the hell with that. Should I back off or jump in your lap?'

'Is there a third option?' Jesse said.

'Of course,' I said. 'I was being a little simplistic.'

Jesse gave Rosie another grape. She was pleased.

'I turned her picture over when I was with you the other night,' Jesse said. 'I wish it were that easy.'

I felt a little tightness in my stomach.

'Jenn?' I said.

'Yes.'

'She's still part of the equation,' I said.

'Yes,' he said. 'But so are you.'

I nodded.

'And, I guess, so is Richie,' I said.

He nodded. I hoped he felt a tightness in his stomach.

'When we started,' Jesse said. 'The other night. We both noticed that it was a time to be careful.'

'And that hasn't changed,' I said.

'But there's something going on here,' Jesse said.

'So we'll proceed,' I said, 'carefully.'

He smiled at me. 'Have you shaved your legs?'

'Yes ...'

'But?'

'But it might be a part of being careful,' I said, 'not to jump into bed every time we're together.'

'It might be,' Jesse said.

'Damn,' I said.

'Damn?'

'Yes,' I said. 'I was hoping you'd talk me out of it.'

'I wish you were wrong,' he said.

'I love having sex with you,' I said, 'and I want to again.'

'Yes,' Jesse said.

'But we have to know we are not just fucking each other to relieve pain.'

'*Fucking* is a one-way verb,' Jesse said. 'We were doing more than fucking.'

'I think we were too,' I said. 'But we need to know that.'

'Yes.'

'So let's not, tonight.'

Jesse nodded.

'Just to see what it's like,' I said.

'To see,' Jesse said.

'I don't want to lose you,' I said.

'I don't think you'll lose me,' Jesse said.

'And I don't think you'll lose me,' I said.

'If we can't survive a sexless evening,' Jesse said. 'We have no future anyway.'

'And if we do survive it, there will be other evenings.'

'Yes,' Jesse said.

'Meanwhile,' I said, 'we can proceed like two professional investigators, working together on a case.'

'You bet,' Jesse said.

We drank some champagne. I looked at Rosie. She did not seem caught up in the conversation.

'Too bad,' Jesse said, 'that you wasted the leg shave, though.'

'It will just make it easier next time,' I said.

43

I felt drained. Jesse was quiet. I couldn't tell what he felt. But it seemed to me we had done something. On the other hand, I knew in moments of strong feeling, things took on meanings that they might not really have. And maybe all we had done was pass on a fun evening…

'What did Captain Cronjager tell you?' I said.

'You met a guy named Sol Hernandez out there?'

'Yes. He went with me to see Gerard.'

'He took an interest in the case' – Jesse smiled – 'or you, and has made it a kind of a hobby, trying to figure out what happened.'

'It was probably me,' I said.

'How could it not be?' Jesse said. 'This started, Cronjager says, right after you were out there. He didn't just start when I called.'

'Sol seemed very intense about things.'

'He is,' Jesse said.

'Could be a good thing or a bad thing,' I said.

'Could be,' Jesse said.

'Intensity can get you in trouble,' I said. 'If you get too involved.'

Jesse smiled.

'Let's stick to this case,' he said. 'Since Sol seems especially intense about Gerard Basgall, for our purposes, it's a good thing.'

'Yes,' I said.

'Case is still open, though Cronjager admits not, ah, very, ah, active, and Sol has talked with the guys assigned, and has been accumulating information, whether it seems to be useful or not.'

'Intensity and patience,' I said. 'That's usually good.'

'Why do I feel we're talking about two things at the same time?' Jesse said.

'Probably because you are a trained and intuitive police officer,' I said.

'And a chief, at that,' Jesse said. 'So Sol's got a big file and there's a lot of stuff in it that seems aimless at the moment – where Basgall went to high school, Erin's gyno, stuff like that. But he also found the law firm that Basgall used when he got busted, or when vice swept up some of his girls.'

'It wasn't Arlo Delaney?' I said.

'Nope. It was an outfit called Jacobson and Fine. The guy that worked on Gerard's cases was the criminal-law guy, Perry Kramer.'

'So?'

'So Sol, being an intense guy, went a little further. He checked the employment records at Jacobson and Fine back five years and there, doing the entertainment-law work, was the late Arlo Delaney, before he left to go into partnership with the late Greg Newton.'

'This is beginning to make my head hurt,' I said.

I got up and got some yellow paper with blue lines and a black Bic pen, and sat down.

'Basgall was Erin and Misty's pimp,' I said, and wrote down the names, 'who had a lawyer who worked in the same firm as Arlo Delaney, who is Moon Monaghan's cousin. Whom he connected to Buddy Bollen to make movies starring Erin, who is pimped by Basgall.'

'Makes sort of a nice circle,' Jesse said.

'It does,' I said. 'Does it tell us who killed Misty?'

'Not yet,' Jesse said.

I looked at my list of names with little arrows I'd drawn connecting them.

'It must lead somewhere,' I said. 'This is just too many coincidental connections.'

'Agreed,' Jesse said. 'But does it take us to who killed Misty?'

'We could look at motive,' I said. 'Buddy owed Moon money. Moon has a history of collecting debts by killing off someone close to the debtor, to scare him.'

'And killing off Erin wouldn't work for Moon,' Jesse said. 'Because if there's a cash cow in Buddy's barn, she's it.'

'And Moon is there, in Boston.'

'So is Buddy,' Jesse said.

'But what is his motive?'

'Because we don't know it,' Jesse said, 'doesn't mean he hasn't got one.'

'Gerard claims he loves Erin,' I said.

'So why would he kill Misty?'

'I don't know,' I said. 'If we could prove that he wasn't in Boston when Misty died, we could eliminate him.'

'Healy is trying to find that out for me,' Jesse said. 'State cops got more resources than the Paradise PD. They're checking airline passenger lists and credit card records.'

'Of course, it could be somebody we don't know anything about and never heard of,' I said.

'Except it would be hard to get in there unannounced with all the security.'

'But not impossible,' I said.

'No. But is it a useful hypothesis for us?' Jesse said.

'No. Does Sol have anything else?'

'Cronjager says that Sol just caught a case involving multiple murders,' Jesse said. 'Maybe a serial killer, high-profile, some celebrities. Misty is on back order for now.'

'So maybe I need to go out there again,' I said.

'Maybe I should go with you,' Jesse said.

'In the continuing spirit of professionalism,' I said.

'You bet,' Jesse said.

'See what we can accomplish when we're not preoccupied with sex,' I said.

'Who's not preoccupied with sex?' Jesse said.

I smiled and finished my glass of champagne.

'Nobody I know,' I said.

44

Grim overcast. Cold sea smell. Logan Airport. American Airlines. 757. Bad lunch. Dumb movie. Neither of us drank. LAX. Hertz. Ford Taurus. 405 northbound. West on Wilshire. Smell of ocean and flowering trees. Temperature 73. No wind.

At 1:11 in the afternoon, we parked the Taurus at a meter in front of a silly-looking cream-colored stucco building on 4th Avenue, at the corner of Wilshire, in Santa Monica, where Jacobson and Fine had offices.

'Is this your first time back?' I said.

He nodded.

'It's the way the air feels,' he said, 'and the way it smells. Isn't like anyplace else.'

'That might be a good thing,' I said.

There was an open two-story elevator shaft in the lobby of the small building, wrought-iron, filigreed and fanciful.

'I liked it here,' Jesse said.

'Except when you didn't.'

'Except then,' Jesse said. 'But that wasn't LA's fault.'

The cute blonde receptionist in the law office wore a hands-free headset and harlequin-shaped glasses with candy-striped frames.

'Stone and Randall,' Jesse said. 'To see Perry Kramer.'

The receptionist relayed that information into her headset.

'You know, actually,' I said, 'not for nothing, but if you were to be alphabetical, it would be Randall and Stone.'

'God,' Jesse said, 'what a blunder.'

A door to the reception room opened and a guy said, 'I'm Perry.'

He was tallish and thin with a short, neat beard and too much black, curly hair. He wore horn-rimmed glasses, like you never see anymore, a flowered shirt, white duck pants, and leather sandals.

'Come on in,' he said.

His office was small, with a view of Wilshire Boulevard. The desk was a maple conference table. On one wall was a large framed picture of a woman with three adolescent girls.

'Randall and Stone,' I said. 'I'm Randall.'

Perry looked at some notes on his desk.

'Sunny,' he said.

'Yes.'

'And Jesse.'

Jesse nodded.

'I'm Perry,' he said. 'You want to talk about Arlo Delaney.'

'For starters,' I said. 'We're also interested in Gerard Basgall.'

'Um-hm,' Perry said.

'Start with Arlo,' Jesse said. 'He worked here?'

'Yeah. Dave Fine – Jacobson's been dead twenty years – Fine wanted to establish an entertainment-law department. I don't know where he found Delaney, but he came cheap, and he was a pretty shrewd guy.'

'Do I hear a *but* in your voice, Perry?' I said.

'But,' Perry said, 'he had the ethical scruples of a fucking tarantula. You don't mind swearing do you, Sunny?'

'I like it,' I said. 'Isn't this the right business, in the right city, for a man with the ethical scruples of a fucking tarantula?'

'Fine's kind of aberrant,' Perry said.

'How about you?' I said.

Perry grinned. 'I'm kind of aberrant, too.'

'Practicing criminal law?' Jesse said.

'That's why I'm in a small office,' Perry said, 'out here at the beach.'

'You ought to be ashamed,' I said.

Perry nodded sadly.

'So,' he said, 'Arlo comes here, and brings a few second-string clients along with him, for starters. Not much, but he hustles, and in time he brings in some names you'd know. We're not talking George Clooney or Julia Roberts here, but some game-show hosts, some television people. He's doing okay. He's billing enough to keep Fine happy.'

'How about Gerard Basgall?' Jesse said.

'How about him?'

'What can you tell us about him?'

'Not much. He used to be a client. There's the confidentiality thing.'

'Sure,' Jesse said. 'Did he know Delaney?'

Perry thought for a moment, apparently saw no conflict, and said, 'Yes. I put them in touch.'

'Because?' I said.

Perry thought some more and then shook his head.

'Perry,' I said. 'I understand the whole lawyer-client thing. We know Gerard is a pimp. We know you represented him and his whores when they were arrested. We know that everybody has a right to the best defense they can get.'

Perry smiled.

'Sadly for them, that was usually me,' Perry said. 'Without acceding to your characterization of them, I did sometimes represent Gerard and some of his female employees in criminal matters.'

'Nicely put,' I said. 'We have a dead woman back home who was once an employee of Gerard Basgall. There is some sort of connection to Arlo Delaney, and we're trying to see if we can close the circle with a connection to Gerard. Do you represent Gerard now?'

'No,' Perry said. 'I knew most of the girls; who was it?'

'Edith Boverini,' Jesse said.

Perry was still for a moment.

Then he said, 'Shit.'

'You knew her,' I said.

'Misty,' he said, 'that was her, ah, professional name.'

'And her sister?' I said.
'Ethel,' Perry said. 'Aka Erin.'
'Do you know who Erin is now?' I said.
'No.'
'Erin Flint.'
Perry was silent a minute, then he said, 'Woman Warrior.'
'That would be Ethel,' I said.
'I'll be damned,' he said.
'You never saw her movies?'
'Oh hell,' Perry said. 'Of course not. What happened to Misty?'
'Somebody broke her neck,' Jesse said.
'With malice aforethought?'
'We believe so,' Jesse said.
Perry was quiet for a moment.
'I liked Misty,' he said.
'And somebody killed Delaney,' I said.
'Yeah, I read that,' Perry said. 'It was a while after he left here to become a mogul.'
'Did he succeed?'
'He and Newton were getting a lot of financing done. I don't think he had made mogul yet.'
'You seem sadder,' I said, 'about Misty.'
Perry nodded.
'I liked Misty,' he said.
'We think Misty's death and Delaney's death may be related,' I said. 'And we want to see where Basgall fits in. Did he know Delaney?'
'Yes,' Perry said.
'Tell me about that.'
Perry nodded thoughtfully.
After some silence he said, 'I introduced them.'
I waited. Jesse was quiet, which I had come to learn was not unusual. One of the things I liked about Jesse was the steady depth of his silence.
'Later,' Perry said, 'if you need to, we can discuss what's on the record, but right now it will be easier if I just talk for your ears only.'
He looked at Jesse. Jesse nodded. He looked at me. I nodded.
'Okay,' he said. 'Gerard's an odd duck. He's a pimp. He's a violent

guy. I'm sure he's killed people. But he also treats the girls better than pimps generally do. I never had any reason to think he slapped them around or didn't pay them fair. And he was always careful about the situations he put them in. If it was hinky, he'd stay right around and make sure they were okay. Some of the violence that got him into trouble and that I had to get him out of was probably against johns who misused Gerard's girls. This was in the early days, when Gerard's enterprise was a hands-on deal. Now he's like a big executive and delegates things. I don't know how the girls do now.'

'A nice pimp,' Jesse said.

'No, Gerard's not nice. He's a mean, arrogant bastard. But he always seemed to like the girls.'

'Most pimps don't,' I said.

'Most pimps hate them,' Perry said. 'But Gerard didn't seem to.'

'All the girls or just the Boverini sisters?'

'All the girls,' Perry said. 'It registered because you never see it much.'

'So why did you hook him up with Delaney?' Jesse said.

'He was looking to get Erin and Misty into the movies.'

'Real movies?' Jesse said.

'Real movies, not porn,' Perry said. 'He asked me if I knew somebody.'

'And you knew Delaney,' Jesse said.

'Yeah. He had left here already, and set up with Newton.'

'What did you think of his idea?'

'The wrong thing,' Perry said. 'He said they were so good-looking he was sure they could make it. I told him they were good-looking, especially Erin. But that beauty was the staple commodity out here. Everybody's beauty queen comes here to be a star.'

'But he insisted they were special,' I said.

'Yeah. I told him he'd probably make more money out of having them fuck rich drunks in luxury hotel suites. Shows you what I know.'

'Maybe you were right,' I said. 'I don't know how much he's made out of her success.'

'She's not with him anymore?'

'No.'

'And Misty is dead. She ever make it?'

'In the movies?' I said. 'Not that I know.'

'Too bad.'

'And you know that he actually hooked up with Delaney,' Jesse said.

'Yes.'

'How about next of kin?' I said.

'He had a wife, Doreen, I think.'

'Got an address?'

'Lemme look,' Perry said.

He didn't have a Rolodex; one point for him. He got an address book from his middle drawer and thumbed through it.

'Last place I got for him,' Perry said, 'is Sherman Oaks.'

He wrote the address on a yellow sticky and handed it to Jesse.

'Know anything else?' I said.

'About Gerard?'

'Yes.'

'Gerard and I had a disagreement, and he left for another lawyer.'

'What did you disagree about?' I said.

'He always lied to me about things,' Perry said. 'I told him I couldn't represent him well if he lied to me.'

'How did he react?'

'He told me I didn't represent him well anyway, and suggested I fuck off.' Perry smiled for a moment. 'Last time I spoke with him.'

'Anything you disagreed about that would help us?'

Perry shook his head slowly.

'No,' he said. 'It was more like … if Gerard gave you the time of day, it would be wise to check with a second source.'

'No wonder he wanted to get into the movie business,' I said.

45

Arlo Delaney's widow lived in a small apartment in a square and graceless white brick apartment building on Woodman Avenue a couple of blocks north of Ventura Boulevard. She acted as if she wasn't happy to see us. But I think she was. It gave her a chance to bitch.

We sat in her stale living room with a view of the Hollywood Freeway. She offered us sherry. We declined. She had some.

'Ever since Arlo . . .' She shook her head. 'It gets harder as the day wears on.'

'I'm sorry for your loss,' Jesse said.

She nodded and looked at her lap.

'Loss,' she said, and sipped some sherry. 'Loss.'

She was a thin woman with pale skin and too much bright makeup. Her blond hair was too short and too colored. It looked brittle. She wore white slacks that were too loose, and a blue-and-yellow flowered blouse with the shirttails tied in front. Her slippers were lined with blue fur.

'I know you have spoken of your husband's death too often,' Jesse said. 'But could you go through it again? We may have some fresh leads on it.'

'What kind of police are you?' she said. 'I forgot what you told me on the phone.'

I was pretty certain that she was not on today's first glass of sherry.

'My name is Jesse Stone,' Jesse said. 'I'm the chief of the Paradise, Massachusetts, Police Department. This is Sunny Randall. She's a detective.'

'You from Massachusetts, too?' Mrs. Delaney said.

'Yes, ma'am,' I said.

She nodded carefully. No one had said I was a police detective. On the other hand, no one had said I wasn't. Her glass was empty.

'Are you sure you won't have some sherry?' she said.

'No thank you,' I said.

Jesse shook his head.

'Sherry's good for you,' Mrs. Delaney said. 'Calms your nerves. Stimulates blood flow.'

She poured herself some more.

'Do you have any thought,' I said, 'about who might have killed your husband and his partner?'

'Do I have a thought? Do I have a *thought*? I don't think of anything else. Five years he's been gone, and I still think about him all the time.'

Jesse nodded. 'Hard business,' he said. 'Who do you think might have done it?'

'I know who did it, for God's sake. I've always known.'

Jesse and I waited. Mrs. Delaney drank some sherry, and swallowed and looked at her lap.

'Who is it?' Jesse said after a while.

'The whore,' she said.

'What is the whore's name?' Jesse said gently.

'She calls herself Erin Flint.'

'The actress,' I said.

'The whore.'

'She calls herself Erin Flint?' Jesse said.

'She's a guinea. Her real name is Boverini.'

'Why did she kill him?' Jesse said.

'Oh, maybe she didn't pull the trigger,' Mrs. Delaney said.

Her glass was empty. She refilled.

'But it was her,' Mrs. Delaney said. 'Hadn't been for her, my Arlo would be alive...'

Tears welled.

'And so would I,' she said.

Her eyes remained moist, but she didn't cry.

'Tell me about her part in it,' Jesse said.

She drank some sherry. There was no hint of impatience in Jesse's manner. We needed to get her pretty soon. In a while she'd be too drunk to talk.

'She got her hooks in Arlo a long time ago. Long before she was Miss Movie Star.'

'They had a relationship?' I said.

'You could call it that, I guess,' Mrs. Delaney said. 'She was fucking him.'

'And you knew that?' I said.

She drank and nodded, looking at her glass. It was a little cut-glass pony. At the rate the sherry was going in, it would have been more efficient to drink from a beer glass.

'I got vaginal dryness,' she said.

Jesse and I both nodded. His face showed nothing.

'So sex is painful for me. Was painful for me.'

She seemed to feel that was sufficient explanation and looked at her sherry glass some more.

'So Arlo went elsewhere for, um, release?' I said.

She nodded. 'I guess I couldn't blame him,' she said to me. 'You know how men are.'

I nodded as if I did. She drank some more sherry.

'It's not like I missed it much anyway,' she said. 'Never did see why everybody made such a big fuss about it.'

'Sex?' I said.

'Yeah. I never thought it was much fun.'

I nodded carefully. Jesse was blank.

'How did he meet her?' I said.

'Erin the whore?' she said. 'His firm represented her pimp. Isn't that a nice business for a law firm, representing pimps and whores.'

'So he knew her pimp?' I said.

'I guess.'

'Did he ever mention the pimp's name?'

'Gerard something,' she said.

'He tell you about him?'

'Later, after he got into trouble.'

'Tell us about the trouble,' Jesse said.

We were both being careful in the way we asked questions. She was the kind of witness who would go wherever you led her, and lie to you because she thought you'd like it. Or because it would enlist your sympathy.

'She wanted to be a movie star,' Mrs. Delaney said.

'Erin Flint,' I said.

Mrs. Delaney nodded and poured some more sherry. She didn't seem to have gotten drunk yet. Maybe she had built a tolerance. Or maybe she was always drunk and had been when we arrived and was just planing on the booze.

'Yes, the whore. And she tried to get Arlo to put her in the movies, and Arlo tells her it's not so easy. And the pimp gets himself involved and I think he threatened Arlo.'

'What did he threaten to do?' I said.

'I don't know. But Arlo was kind of scared.'

'And?' I said.

'And nothing. Arlo didn't like to talk about it, her being his whore and stuff ... didn't keep him from doing it, a'course.'

'So do you think it was Gerard who killed him and his partner?' Jesse said.

'I don't know. But it was because of the whore, I know that.'

'How?' Jesse said.

'Because I'm a woman,' Mrs. Delaney said. 'A wife and a woman. And a woman knows other women.'

Jesse looked at me without expression.

'Absolutely,' I said. 'Did you tell the Los Angeles police this?'

'Of course not,' she said.

'But you're telling us,' I said.

'I can talk to a woman,' she said.

'The other detectives were men?' I said.

'Detective Sanchez,' she said with an exaggerated accent. 'And Detective Munoz. Do you think I'm going to sit here with two muchachos and talk about vaginal dryness?'

I glanced at Jesse.

'It's good I came along,' I said.

46

'She ever hear of K-Y gel?' Jesse said when we were riding back through Beverly Glen.

'I'm not sure it would have made much difference.'

'She didn't like it anyway,' Jesse said.

'Erin might not have been the first,' I said. 'You think there's anything to what she says?'

'It doesn't contradict anything we know,' Jesse said.

'Her brain is pretty well pickled,' I said.

'And it hasn't given her a sunny outlook.'

'You're just mad because she doesn't like men,' I said.

'That's probably it,' Jesse said.

At the foot of Beverly Glen we turned left onto Sunset. It was the Beverly Hills expensive part of Sunset, and got more so as we drove east toward Rodeo Drive.

'It's like we're in a maze,' I said. 'Every time we talk to a new person we get more information that leads us nowhere.'

Jesse nodded. We turned down Rodeo Drive. It was early evening by now, after sundown. The lights in the luxury homes were clearly visible in the gathering darkness. I was driving through Beverly Hills, headed for a luxury hotel with a man whom I found very attractive. We had not had romantic contact since we slept together three thousand miles east. Jesse had been pleasant and professional and easy, as if we were friends, which we were fast becoming, more than lovers, which we had already been, at least once. Despite the easiness and the professionalism, however, there was between us a kind of erotic tension that we both accepted without comment. We both knew we'd revisit it.

We crossed Santa Monica Boulevard and little Santa Monica, and drove through the implausibly chic shopping area to the Beverly Wilshire. We were both on expenses.

'Does police travel in Paradise usually include hotels like this?'

'They do for the chief,' Jesse said.

'Who approves the travel expenses?' I said.

'The chief,' Jesse said.

We gave the car to the valet and went into the lobby.

'Want a drink?' Jesse said.

'As long as it's not sherry,' I said.

We turned right into the bar and sat at a small table. The unremarked tension between us became a little more insistent. Jesse had a tall scotch and soda. I got a Cosmopolitan. We touched glasses. The bar was nearly two-thirds full. It was a good-looking crowd, well-dressed generally, and not loud. I always liked not loud.

'I suppose the next stop is your pimp friend,' Jesse said.

'My friend?'

'You've met him,' Jesse said. 'I haven't.'

'Okay,' I said. 'We talk to my pimp friend. It will not be an easy conversation. My pimp friend is not cop-friendly.'

'Cronjager feels bad because he had to fire me,' Jesse said. 'He'll provide us a jurisdictional presence.'

'Wow,' I said. 'A jurisdictional presence?'

Jesse nodded.

'Now and then I impress myself,' he said.

We were quiet, sipping our drinks, looking at our fellow drinkers. There was nothing ill at ease in our quiet. But the unobtrusive force of the tension tightened. We had another drink. I looked at my watch. Six-twenty.

'I assume we are off duty,' I said.

'We are,' Jesse said.

'So we are now just a couple of pals sitting around having drinks together.'

'Yes.'

'There is a boutique I have always wanted to go to,' I said.

'A boutique?'

'I've been out here half a dozen times and I've never been.'

'A boutique?' Jesse said.

'It's open until nine tonight.'

'All of a sudden you've turned into a girl?' Jesse said.

'I've done that before,' I said.

Jesse smiled.

'I remember,' he said. 'What's the store?'

'Jere Jillian,' I said.

'In Beverly Hills?' he said.

'Right up the street.'

'And you'd like me to go with you?'

'I would,' I said.

Jesse grinned.

'Is it fabulous?' he said.

'Fabulous,' I said.

47

I felt odd walking up Rodeo Drive with Jesse. Of course, walking up Rodeo Drive with anyone is odd. Rodeo Drive is odd, the logical result of intersecting movies and fashion.

'This is ridiculous,' Jesse said.

'I know,' I said. 'Don't you love it?'

'Fabulous,' Jesse said.

There were a lot of couples looking in windows of idiotically chic stores. Many were Asian tourists. And I realized what the odd feeling was. Jesse and I felt like a couple. I looked at him. If he felt it too, he wasn't showing anything. That didn't mean much; as far as I could tell, Jesse never showed anything. Almost never.

Jere Jillian was all glass and stainless steel. Anything that was neither was white. In the window was a huge blowup of a glamorous woman purported to be Jere herself. There were a few dresses in very small sizes hanging on display. Several perfectly dressed saleswomen in tight clothes and very high heels stood around, trying not to laugh at my attire. Several other customers moved reverently among the garments, closely attended by a salesperson.

'Place looks like a whorehouse,' Jesse murmured.

'But a very elegant one,' I said.

The nearest saleswoman accosted me as soon as I was through the door. The others not with customers lingered in place, smiling at Jesse, covertly checking themselves in the many mirrors. My salesperson had long, honey-blond hair that fell forward on one side of her face and covered one eye, like an old movie star whose name I couldn't remember.

'Are you lookin' for anything special?' she said.

And so it began. Jesse sat quietly in a low, white chair that appeared uncomfortable and watched me. I hadn't shopped with a man since Richie. I felt myself almost wallowing in it. Except for the exotica of my surroundings, it seemed so normal. There were two other men sitting with equal boredom and discomfort. Shopping Rodeo Drive isn't pretty.

My salesperson's name was Amber. Of course.

'Oh, that's perfect for you... Look at yourself... I have just exactly the shoes for that dress... What do you think, sir? ... Doesn't she look fabulous?'

'Fabulous,' Jesse said.

Finally we had narrowed my selections down to three, and it was time to try on. During the narrowing process, Jesse had sat motionless in his uncomfortable chair and said nothing except an occasional 'Fabulous' when asked. He seemed content, but there was something in his face, some brightness that made me wonder about him. We'd had two drinks each before we came to Jere Jillian, so it wasn't that he was drunk.

The dressing room was small, with the kind of saloon doors that leave your feet visible as you changed. The floor had a good carpet. There was a small bench and a lovely three-way mirror. Jere had class. Amber hung my selections on a hook and backed out.

'I'll be right outside,' Amber said. 'Call me if you need anything.'

The first dress I tried wouldn't do, and I knew that immediately when it was on me. But the other two I couldn't decide. I tried each one twice, and then, wearing one of the two contenders, I called Amber. She opened the door immediately. I handed her the reject dress.

'I've got it down to two,' I said.

'You're absolutely right,' Amber said. 'This one isn't quite right for you, now that I see you in that one.'

'You can put that one back,' I said, 'and would you ask the man I'm with to step over here?'

'Of course,' Amber said. 'He's so good, sitting there so patient.'

'He is,' I said.

Amber hustled off, and I stood in the door of the dressing room in one of the two dresses. When Jesse arrived, I stood on the balls of my feet to simulate heels.

'Pretend that my bra straps aren't showing,' I said. 'What do you think?'

'Fabulous,' Jesse said.

'No, really. It's important to me; I can't decide.'

'You look beautiful in it,' Jesse said.

I turned around.

'How about the back?'

'Front and back,' Jesse said. 'Beautiful.'

I had been naked with this man, had sex with him. But somehow this ritual moment seemed the most intimate thing we'd done. I almost blushed.

'Is it at all too tight around my butt?' I said.

'No.'

Our eyes met for a moment, and I realized that he felt the intimacy, too.

'Okay, stay right there,' I said. 'I'm going to try on the other one.'

I closed the door and slipped the dress up over my head, trying to be careful of my hair. The door opened behind me. I slid the dress off and looked and it was Jesse.

'I'm in my underwear,' I said.

'Flesh-toned,' Jesse said.

'Appropriate under light, Southern California clothes,' I said. 'Why are you in here?'

'I thought it was time for us to have sex again,' Jesse said.

The room was small. He was very close.

'Here?' I said.

'Yes.'

'In Jere Jillian?'

'Uh-huh.'

'In the dressing room?' I said.

'The very place,' Jesse said

He put his arms around me.

'Standing up against the wall?' I said.

Jesse glanced briefly around the room.

'Seems our best bet,' he said.

'With Amber lurking outside?'

'Adds to the excitement,' Jesse said. 'And, as a special feature, this perfectly situated three-way mirror.'

'We'd be fools not to, I guess.'

'Fools,' Jesse said.

'But *quietly*!' I said.

I giggled. He kissed me. I kissed him back. We pressed together. He began to help me with my underpants. And then we were fully engaged. We were both agile and strong. Standing up was okay. The three-way mirror showed me a Sunny Randall I had never quite seen before. It made me uneasy. But it was sort of interesting.

Outside the dressing-room door, Amber said, 'Do you need any help?'

I held myself still inside to answer her.

'No thanks,' I said in a perfectly normal voice.

'Is it too big, at all?' Amber said. 'I have a smaller size.'

'Oh,' I said, 'God no. If anything it might be a little small.'

In my ear Jesse whispered, 'Hey!'

'I could get you a size larger,' Amber said.

With Jesse pressed against me, I could feel him shake with repressed laughter. I laughed too. And pressed together, fully connected, standing up and moving against the wall, with Amber lurking hopefully outside the door, we giggled covertly together in an intimacy I had never shared with anyone.

48

I never did try on the other dress. I bought the one I had tried on, for far more than I should have spent. I tried not to blush while Amber put my credit card through. If Jesse was ill at ease, he concealed it. He leaned on the jamb of the front door while he waited. Amber smiled as she put my dress in a silver garment bag with *Jere Jillian* written across it in lavender script.

'Thanks so much for coming in,' she said. 'I hope you have a fabulous night.'

From his spot at the door Jesse said, 'Fabulous.'

I glanced back through the big glass window as we left and saw Amber talking with two other saleswomen. Were they laughing? About us? Or was I imagining it?

'I feel like I've just been in a porn film,' I said to Jesse as we walked back down Rodeo Drive toward the hotel.

'Kind of fun,' Jesse said.

'Only kind of?'

'Cop understatement,' Jesse said. 'It is probably the most fun I've ever had.'

'Me too,' I said.

We were quiet for a while.

'I wonder what Amber thought,' I said.

'That's part of the fun,' Jesse said. 'Wondering what she thought.'

'She could see our feet below the dressing-room doors,' I said.

'If she looked,' Jesse said.

'She could see my underpants,' I said.

'Around one ankle, as I recall,' Jesse said.

'That might raise her suspicions,' I said.

'Perhaps,' Jesse said, 'we can never shop at Jere Jillian again.'

'I couldn't afford to go back anyway,' I said.
'Maybe we ought to organize a hobby for ourselves,' Jesse said.
'Having sex in public?' I said.
'Just a thought,' Jesse said.
'If we made a habit of it, it would cease to be special,' I said.
'Good point,' Jesse said.
We crossed Wilshire at the light and went into the hotel lobby.
'What would you like to do about supper?' Jesse said.
'I'd like us to have room service together,' I said.
'Your place or mine?' Jesse said.
'Your room is bound to be neater,' I said.
'Almost certainly,' Jesse said.
We were alone in the elevator.
'You know what I like especially about our, ah, frolic in Jere Jillian? It sort of relaxed everything. Sex was not a moment of intense and ponderous passion.'
'It was not, on the other hand, dispassionate,' Jesse said.
'No. But it was fun. Sex is often fun, and probably should be undertaken sometimes just for that reason.'
'Because it's fun?' Jesse said.
'Uh-huh.'
The elevator stopped. The doors opened and we got out.
'And you,' Jesse said as we walked down the hall, 'a native Bostonian.'
He opened his door and we went in. His room was in fact far neater than mine would ever be.
'Don't ever rat me out,' I said, 'to the Harvard Club.'

49

Captain Cronjager went with us to see Gerard Basgall. He and his driver picked us up in a big, black Crown Victoria. Cronjager sat in front. Jesse and I in the back. Cronjager turned sideways in the front seat to talk with us.
'Chance to visit with you,' he said to Jesse. 'And it's nice to do a little fieldwork now and again.'

'Elaine is used to running the show anyway,' Jesse said, 'when you're out of the office.'

Cronjager smiled.

'Or when I'm not,' he said.

The driver laughed. He was a large, pleasant-looking black man with a neat mustache.

Cronjager said, 'No need to be laughing at your commanding officer, Clyde.'

'Laughing with you, Captain,' Clyde said. 'Laughing with you.'

We parked in front of Gerard's huge house. Clyde opened the door for Cronjager and came around in time to hold the door for me.

'Want I should come in, Captain,' Clyde said.

'Nope,' Cronjager said. 'Wait for us here. Unless you hear me scream. Then you come running.'

'Yessir,' Clyde said and leaned his considerable self against the car.

The same fat guy with a similar flowered shirt opened the front door and gave us the same fish-eyed stare.

'I know you, Blondie,' he said to me. 'Who are these guys?'

'Cronjager,' the Captain said and held up his badge.

'A freakin' captain,' the fat guy said. 'First fucking class.'

We sat in the same room that Sol and I had sat in on my last visit. Cronjager sat a little to the side. Gerard was all in white today, looking clean and polished.

'My name's Cronjager,' the captain said. 'Sunny you know. He's Jesse Stone.'

Gerard nodded and didn't say anything.

'I'm the chief of police in Paradise, Massachusetts,' Jesse said.

Gerard said, 'I'm glad for you, Jesse.'

'We like you for Misty Taylor,' Jesse said.

'You what?'

'We like you for the murder,' Jesse said. 'We think you did her.'

'Why do you think that?' Gerard said.

'Your name keeps coming up,' Jesse said.

Gerard smiled.

'Popular guy,' he said.

'We're checking transportation,' Jesse said. 'If you were in

Boston any time that matters, we're going to know it.'

'How many cops you got in Paradise, Massachusetts?' Gerard said.

'Counting school crossing guards?' Jesse said. 'Fifteen.'

'Be taking you some time to do that checking, won't it? What with all them tickets to write,' Gerard said. 'All them kids to bust for smoking mary-ju-wanna.'

'We're getting some help from the state police,' Jesse said.

Gerard nodded.

'Good for you,' Gerard said.

Cronjager was silent. He was watching Jesse. He wanted to see if Jesse was all right. I smiled a little to myself, thinking of how, in at least one area, I could reassure him.

'Here's how we figure,' Jesse said. 'It's hard to buy a pimp falling for one of his whores, but say you did. Erin wanted to be something more than an upscale hooker. You wanted to help her. So you talked to Perry Kramer, and he put you in touch with Arlo Delaney, who by now was running a film-financing operation. Arlo brings in his cousin, guy named Moon Monaghan, who's looking for something to do with a lot of cash, and wants to be a movie mogul. And one way or another, Arlo, or you, or both of you find Buddy Bollen, and use the financing you already got to sell Erin to him.'

I was quiet. This was Jesse's show. With Cronjager in the audience.

'Erin might have even helped persuade somebody,' Jesse said.

Gerard looked thoughtfully at Jesse for a time without speaking. Then he said, 'She fucked all of them. So did Misty.'

'All of them being?'

'Arlo, Buddy, Moon. She's still fucking Buddy.'

I couldn't contain myself.

'Moon?' I said.

'Yep. She and Misty. A twosome. Like with Buddy.'

I was struggling with the concept of anyone sleeping with Moon.

'Misty and Erin?' Jesse said. 'Both sleeping with Buddy.'

'Yeah,' Gerard said.

'Even after the movies got made?'

'Part of the deal,' Gerard said.

The fat guy leaned on the wall near the French doors. Off to the side, Cronjager sat with his legs crossed. He appeared to be looking at the backs of his hands.

'Talk about the deal,' Jesse said.

Gerard glanced over at the fat man by the French doors.

'Packy,' he said. 'Take a walk.'

The fat man nodded and left the room.

'Buddy would take the money from Arlo's cousin,' Gerard said, 'and he'd make the movie and put Erin in it. But they both had to stay with him, and do him whenever he wanted.'

'Both ... ?'

'Erin and Misty.'

'What if they stopped doing him?' Jesse said.

'End of career,' Gerard said.

'I'm not sure she needs him anymore,' I said.

'Maybe not, but she thinks she does,' Gerard said. 'Besides, there's that baseball thing.'

'She cares about that?' Jesse said.

'She wants to be important,' Gerard said, 'for more than tits and ass. She wants to be a female Jackie Robinson.'

Jesse looked at me. I nodded.

'What did Misty get out of it?'

'Money. Erin shared the wealth.'

'Did Misty want to be a contendah?' I said.

'I don't know,' Gerard said.

'Is Erin straight?' I said.

Gerard looked at me for a moment.

'I ain't been renting her out to women,' he said.

'You know as well as I do,' I said to Gerard, 'that some whores are lesbians.'

'For them it's strictly business,' Gerard said. 'For Erin and Misty it was business and pleasure.'

'They liked the work?' I said.

'Yeah.'

'You're sure?' I said.

Gerard smiled at me. It was a nasty smile.

'I'm sure,' Gerard said.

'Both of them?'

'Uh-huh.'

'You seem pretty current,' Jesse said, 'about Erin.'

'We kept in touch.'

'When's the last time you saw her?' Jesse said.

Gerard leaned back a little in his chair. The California sunshine flooded into the atrium. Gerard clasped his hands in front of his chin, his elbows on the arms of the chair. He smiled a little. His teeth were bright and perfect. His hair was expensively cut. His skin was smooth and tan. His neck was strong. His hands were manicured. His white shirt was crisp. His white trousers were creased.

'Day before Misty died,' he said.

Cronjager uncrossed his legs and recrossed them the other way. It was nice that he was still so limber. Jesse showed nothing. Showing nothing was one of the things Jesse did best. I felt myself tighten a little in my chair.

'You'd have found it anyway,' Gerard said. 'American Airlines, both ways. First class, of course. Limo from the airport.'

'Where'd you stay?' Jesse said.

'Not in Paradise,' Gerard said. 'Nice town you got there, Chief. I seen more people in Ralphs market in West LA.'

'So where?' Jesse said.

His voice was quiet in the still room.

'Boston,' Gerard said. 'Four Seasons. What's the difference?'

'Better to know than not know,' Jesse said. 'What did you go to see Erin for?'

'Visit,' Gerard said.

'Why?'

'Old times' sake,' Gerard said. 'Remember I told you I love her? I visit every month or so.'

'What did you do while you were there?'

'Same as always,' Gerard said. 'We visited.'

'I need more than that,' Jesse said.

'I don't have more than that,' Gerard said. 'I picked her up in the limo, took her to Boston, we visited for a day.'

'At the hotel.'

'Yeah.'

'Buddy know about your visit?'
'Hell no,' Gerard said.
'And then you went home?'
'Yeah, like always,' Gerard said. 'Brought her back next day. Came back to LA the day after, noon flight, gets in to LA about three.'
'That would be the day after Misty was killed.'
'I guess,' Gerard said. 'I didn't know it at the time.'
'And now you do,' Jesse said.
Gerard turned his palms up.
'Got nothing to do with me,' he said.
'What limo company?' Jesse said.
'Carey.'
'You have any thoughts on who killed Misty?' Jesse said.
'All I know is, I didn't.'
'We'll check this,' Jesse said.
'You would have anyway,' Gerard said.
'Which is why you told us.'
'Exactly,' Gerard said.

50

We got nothing else from Gerard, though it wasn't for lack of trying. And when we finally left, we'd been there at least two hours longer than we needed to be.
'Well,' I said, 'he was there.'
'So was Moon,' Jesse said. 'And Buddy.'
'And Erin,' I said.
Clyde was driving us down Hilgard past UCLA. Beside him in the front seat, Cronjager was admiring the campus, and maybe the coeds.
'Don't know the case like you do,' Cronjager said, still looking at the campus. 'And, a'course, I'm not a chief of police, but I didn't hear him tell you anything you can use to nail him.'
'If he needs to be nailed,' I said.
'You think he doesn't?' Cronjager said.

'He needs to be nailed for being a pimp and a thug,' I said. 'But I'm not convinced he did it.'

'Because?' Jesse said.

'Because he doesn't feel right for it,' I said.

'Woman's intuition?' Jesse said.

'Woman cop's intuition,' I said. 'The perfect combination.'

'Talk about it a little,' Jesse said.

'You know as well as I do that a lot of what we know isn't fact. It's how people look and act when we talk to them. It's how we feel about the way they sound and what they do with their eyes.'

Jesse nodded.

'We frequently know who the perp is before we can prove it,' he said. 'You got any favorites?'

'No,' I said. 'But we know one thing.'

'Erin?' Jesse said.

In front of me I saw Cronjager nod his head. Jesse wasn't looking at him.

'Yes,' I said. 'Erin. She knew Gerard was in Boston and didn't tell us.'

'So what else does she know that she hasn't told us?' Jesse said.

'When I get home, I'll ask her,' I said. 'Woman to woman.'

'Sisterhood is strong,' Jesse said.

'Do you buy that stuff about her wanting to be a female Jackie Robinson?' Cronjager said.

'Yes,' I said. 'I think I do.'

'You seen her play, Jesse?' Cronjager said.

'I've seen her hit,' Jesse said.

'Can she make it?' I said.

'Sure. It's Buddy's team; he can put her out there and they gotta let her play.'

'But?'

'She'll be humiliated,' Jesse said. 'She can't generate the bat speed. Unless some nitwit throws her a changeup, she may strike out every time.'

'Thus proving that women can't in fact play baseball with the men,' I said.

'There may be some who can,' Jesse said. 'I don't know. But it is not Erin.'

'Could those college boys strike her out?' I said.

'Sure. Taft's got a good program for a Northern school. They were in the College World Series three years ago. Kid's location may not be precise. I don't know what they got for a breaking ball. And I don't know how much movement they get off the fastball. But the kid I saw can throw it by her.'

'Could they strike you out?'

'Now? Sure.'

'When you were playing.'

'Not often,' Jesse said.

The car was quiet. Clyde took us up a hill to Selby Avenue, and left onto Wilshire.

'You got a plan?' Jesse said after a time.

'I'm thinking about one,' I said.

'You want to prove to her she can't do it?' Jesse said.

'Maybe,' I said.

'Give her less to protect,' Jesse said.

'Soften her up before I question her,' I said.

Jesse smiled at me.

He said, 'You are a hard case, Sunny Randall.'

I shrugged.

'If you're right,' I said, 'it's better she knows it now.'

We went down the corridor of high-rise condos, past the country club. Century City soared in the near distance beyond the club.

'Remember,' Cronjager said from the front seat. 'I got an unsolved double homicide out here that your case has something to do with.'

'I'll keep it in mind,' Jesse said.

We went up the hill toward Beverly Glen. There was no one on the street except a couple of Hispanic gardeners, working out of an ancient maroon pickup, grooming a small front lawn.

'You and Jenn doing anything these days?' Cronjager said.

'Jenn's doing something,' Jesse said. 'But not with me.'

Cronjager nodded, still looking out his side window as if he'd never seen Los Angeles before.

'I heard she's back east where you are,' Cronjager said.

'Yes.'

'How's your general health?' Cronjager said.
'I'm not getting drunk very often,' Jesse said.
'Okay, so I can talk in front of Sunny?' Cronjager said.
'Yes.'
'You over Jenn?' Cronjager said.
I felt myself tighten up a little.
'I think so,' Jesse said.
'And you're sober.'
'Reasonably,' Jesse said.
'I'm glad to see it,' Cronjager said. 'You're a good cop, and a good man. I hated firing you.'
We approached the Beverly Hilton, near where Wilshire and Santa Monica intersect.
'You had no choice, Captain,' Jesse said.
'No,' Cronjager said. 'I didn't.'

51

It was winter in Paradise. And the recency of LA made it seem more so. The gym at Taft was sort of gloomy. Erin was in the batting cage. The big kid who had pitched to her the first time I'd seen her hit was standing on the pitcher's mound. This time there was a catcher, too, in his catcher's outfit, squatting behind the plate. Someone had taken away the little batting-practice fence that had been there before. Roy Linden leaned against the cage, watching.
'Be a simulated game,' Linden said to Erin. 'I'll call balls and strikes from behind the cage. Won't be right on it, but you'll get an idea. Pitcher's going to try to get you out. You going to just make contact. Line drive is a hit. Ground ball or pop-up is an out. No need to hit it to New Hampshire.'
Erin nodded. She had on cobalt shorts and top with a matching headband. She was wearing spikes. Linden moved directly behind Erin, with the batting-cage screen to protect him.
'You discussed this with Mr. Linden?' I said to Jesse.
'Yes. He liked it. He's pretty sick of Erin.'

Linden pointed at the pitcher.

'Play ball,' he said with the hint of a smile.

'And he's discussed it with the pitcher?' I said.

'The pitcher will be trying to get her out. Linden told him, nothing fancy. Fastballs should do it.'

'Linden agrees with you that she won't be able to hit?'

'Yes.'

The pitcher threw. Erin didn't swing. The ball cracked into the catcher's mitt. Erin turned and looked at Linden.

'That's a strike, Erin,' Linden said.

She turned back, set her feet again. Swung the bat again.

I said, 'My God, Jesse, she can't hit that.'

'True.'

'Nobody could hit that.'

'They could,' Jesse said. 'It comes fast but it's straight. No movement.'

The next pitch came just as fast. Erin swung this time and didn't hit it.

'And you could hit that?' I said. 'When you were playing?'

'Sure.'

'And you weren't even a great hitter,' I said.

'No. I hit enough to survive. But I was going to make it with my glove and my arm.'

The ball cracked into the catcher's mitt again. Erin had swung and missed badly.

'Find his release point,' Linden said to her. 'Pick up the ball coming out of his hand.'

Erin nodded. Staring out at the pitcher, she crouched a little more in her batting position. I thought the pitcher had a little smile on his face. But I wasn't close enough to be sure. He pitched. She swung and missed.

'I can't see the rotation,' Erin said to Linden.

'Don't worry about rotation,' Linden said. 'He's throwing nothing but fastballs.'

Pitch. Swing. Miss. I could feel it in my stomach. This was awful.

'And this pitcher couldn't make the big leagues?'

'Guys like Barry Bonds,' Jesse said, 'Manny Ramirez, would hit .800 off this kid. They'd pay his salary to keep him in the league.'

Pitch. Swing. Miss.

'This is awful,' I said to Jesse.

'Hard game,' he said. 'It's one of the things about sports. It's clean. Either you can do it or you can't.'

'Not just sports,' I said.

'No, a lot of skill things. Ballet. Singing. Whatever. You may get further than your talent allows because somebody like Buddy comes along and packages you and sneaks you around the hurdles. But you still can't *do* it. Things have their rules.'

Pitch. Swing. Miss.

'Like love,' I said.

'I thought all was fair in love,' Jesse said.

'You can love someone however much, and if they don't love you, you can't make them.'

'They can't love you because you want them to,' Jesse said.

'I know.'

'Mutual interests help,' Jesse said.

'Like being in the same profession?' I said.

Jesse smiled.

'Like that,' he said.

Erin swung and missed and threw the bat away and began to cry. The rest of us in the gym seemed to freeze. The pitcher and catcher were motionless.

'Oh God,' I whispered to Jesse.

'I can't hit it,' Erin said, crying. 'I can't hit it. I can't hit it. I can't fucking hit it.'

Linden's voice was gentle, but the gym was so still that it carried. He said, 'No, Erin. You can't.'

52

Dr Silverman was in black today. Black sweater, black suit. She had on a small silver necklace. She gleamed with grooming, in, of course, an understated way. As I talked she watched me with complete attention, apparently absorbed by everything I said, every hand gesture, every shift in my position.

'With my pants down,' I said. 'In a public dressing room on Rodeo Drive.'

Dr Silverman nodded.

'I mean, my God,' I said.

She nodded again. I didn't quite know what I was trying to say.

'Have you ever done anything like that?' I said.

I knew the question was inane as it slipped out. She smiled. She knew it was inane and she knew I knew it.

'Why do you ask?' she said.

'I know, I know,' I said. 'It's about me, not about you.'

'But why do you ask?' she said.

I thought.

'I probably asked it so you'd push me to examine my own reactions,' I said.

'Talk about that,' she said.

'I feel, or maybe I feel, like a whore, you know? I mean, that wasn't lovemaking. That was … that was just fucking.'

'Define "fucking,"' she said.

'I suppose I have some sense of it as exploiting a partner for your own pleasure. Not having sex because you love them.'

'Like you and Tony Gault?'

She didn't forget anything.

'No, that was just for fun.'

She nodded.

'I don't love Tony.'

She nodded and raised her eyebrows. I knew that meant *So?* in shrink sign language.

'Maybe I am starting to love Jesse.'

She nodded.

'And it scares me. If I will do that, what's next? Sex in Harvard Square? At noon?'

'So you're worried about the sex?' she said.

'Sure … no … of course not. I'm worried about losing control. About loving him too much and giving myself over to him.'

'And at the moment you were worrying about loss of control, you had this exotic sexual experience.'

I nodded. She nodded. She raised her eyebrows again. I didn't know what to say.

'Sometimes,' she said, 'we dramatize our interior state by what we do.'

We sat. I studied her face. I couldn't tell how old she was, except I knew she was older than I.

'So, my experience tells me that being in love with someone may make me submerge myself…' I said.

She nodded slightly. That meant *Go ahead*.

'And then we have sex in a store, and I fasten my fears onto that.'

She nodded. I sat. And then there it was. I saw it all, in full, at once, like turning on a light.

'I have always thought,' I said, 'that if you were in love, the only purpose of sex was to express that love, and anything else was fucking.'

'There's a lot at stake,' she said.

'A lot,' I said. 'Every time you have sex, it has to prove you love each other.'

'Freighted with anxiety,' she said.

'Unless you don't love each other,' I said.

She nodded.

'Then it's easy,' I said.

'Sex is better with someone you don't love?' she said.

'Yes,' I said. 'No. Both.'

She raised her eyebrows.

'Well, I mean, it's easier in some ways if there's just sort of a friendship. No big deal. Nothing to prove. Have a nice time,' I said. 'But on the other hand, it lacks something. With someone you love, it's not just fun, it's … important.'

'Good news and bad news,' she said.

I listened to my breathing for a while.

'I suppose,' I said, 'that if I were fully, ah, integrated, I could seek the pleasure and let the love take care of itself. You know, I mean, lovemaking isn't just sex. If you love someone you are making love all the time. When you talk. When you eat dinner together. When you laugh or walk along. And when you are having sex.'

'And if the sex isn't what you'd hoped for?'

'It doesn't mean we don't make love.'

She smiled at me.

'Sometimes,' she said, 'the fish just don't bite.'

Wow. She's approving. I felt empowered.

'What if there were no sex?' I said.

She shook her head ever so slightly, as if diminishing the gesture made it less directive.

'Sex is part of love,' she said.

'Do you believe in love?' I said.

I knew it was a question she would probably turn aside. Much too intimate a revelation for a shrink to make to a patient. *Why do you ask?* she would say. Or she'd paraphrase. *There are certainly strong emotions centered on relational blah blah …*

'Yes,' she said. 'I do.'

53

I met Erin Flint for lunch at the Bristol Lounge in the Four Seasons Hotel. No bodyguards. No entourage. No Buddy. Just Erin, who turned every head when she walked in and came across to my table by the window. Up close, her face looked tired and sort of tight.

I stood to shake hands with her and found myself putting my arms around her. She felt stiff.

'No bodyguards?' I said.

'No. They're for Buddy,' she said. 'He pretends it's me. But it's him. He's scared of something.'

'What?'

'I have no idea,' Erin said.

'You okay?' I said.

She shook her head.

'You were there,' she said. 'With the local cop.'

'Yesterday? Yes. That was awful for you.'

'I bet the men liked it,' she said.

'I don't think they did,' I said.

'You don't know men like I do,' she said.

'Perhaps not,' I said.

A waitress arrived. Erin asked for white wine. I ordered iced tea.

'Buddy still wants me to do it,' she said. 'He says even if I'm not Jackie Robinson I can still be Eddie Gaedel.'

'Who's Eddie Gaedel?'

'A midget that batted once for the Saint Louis Browns and walked. It was a publicity stunt.'

I didn't say anything.

'I've made five movies that did really well. I been in *People* magazine, and *Entertainment Weekly.* I was on *Late Night with Conan O'Brien…*'

The wine and iced tea came. Erin drank some of her wine at once. I remained calm about my iced tea.

'And he wants me to be a fucking publicity stunt,' she said.

'How do you feel about that?' I said.

'I want to go someplace and sit in a hole.'

'Maybe you should get out of all this,' I said.

'He knew, didn't he?' Erin said. 'That cop.'

'Chief Stone,' I said. 'Yes. He used to play baseball.'

'And Roy knew?'

I nodded.

'It was Buddy's idea,' she said. 'You know? When he bought that baseball team. He had a great genius moment. He hired Roy Linden to teach me. He invented a past for me about playing softball and all that crap.'

'You never played?' I said.

'No. Not until they started teaching me.'

'In your life?' I said.

'No.'

'My God,' I said, 'Erin. You look like you've played all your life. Do you realize what an accomplishment that is?'

She shook her head.

'I was never going to make it. A woman's got no chance.'

'Most people never make it,' I said. 'Most don't get to where you were. Man or woman.'

'Yeah, sure.'

She got another glass of wine.

'I need to talk with you about Gerard,' I said.

Erin nodded. I knew how she felt. She wanted to be in her hole, far away, alone. She didn't care what I wanted to talk about.

'Gerard set most of this up,' I said.

She nodded absently and looked out the window onto Boylston

Street. There was light snow falling. It was melting on the roadway and collecting a little on the grassy areas of the Public Garden across the street.

'Part of the deal,' I said, 'was you and Misty had to sleep with Buddy.'

'"Sleep with" is a nice way to say it,' Erin said. 'He liked it that we were sisters.'

'Was it unpleasant?'

'It still is,' Erin said. 'And now I got to do it alone.'

'You don't love Buddy?'

I felt foolish asking, but I didn't know how else to ask.

'Buddy's a pig,' Erin said.

'But it was part of the deal?' I said.

'Uh-huh.'

'It must have been unpleasant,' I said.

She nodded.

'Thing about being a whore,' she said. 'You fuck a lot of pigs. You learn tricks. Make them think you like it. Keep yourself out of it, you know? So it doesn't, you know, register in your head.'

'Are you straight, Erin?'

'I guess so,' she said. 'I banged a thousand guys and no women.'

She drank some wine. She did not make eye contact. She stared out at the snow falling pleasantly on the Public Garden.

'Did you enjoy any of them?' I said.

I wasn't sure where the conversation was going. I wasn't sure it was entirely about Erin, either.

'Gerard,' she said.

'Your pimp.'

She nodded.

'He slept with Misty as well?' I said.

'Yeah, sure, but not at the same time.'

It was snowing harder in the Back Bay. But it wasn't a driving snow. It was the kind of snow that would probably stop in a few hours and would never accumulate all that much. The streets would be clear, and the city would look pretty until the snow got dirty.

'Gerard was here,' I said, 'in Boston, during the time Misty was killed.'

She looked at me for the first time.

'He was?' she said.

'You know he was,' I said. 'He came to see you.'

She looked at me. I waited. She looked out at the snowfall. Then she looked at me again.

'I didn't want to get him in trouble,' she said.

54

There was no snow in Paradise. Along the North Shore it had been rain. Jesse and I were in the empty squad room at Paradise police headquarters. The back window overlooked the parking lot and the Highway Department maintenance shed. There were empty coffee cups and the remnants of a submarine sandwich on the conference table. There was a big chalkboard on one wall. Jesse stood beside it. I sat at the far end of the conference table.

'Her story matches Gerard's,' I said.

'Which means either it's true or they concocted it together.'

'Correct,' I said.

Jesse walked the length of the conference room and stared out the back window. Then he turned and walked to the other end of the room and turned and looked at me.

'She was there with no security.'

'Which means she could have gone off with Gerard when he was here, also without security,' Jesse said.

'She says the security is really for Buddy. He pretends it's for her.'

'So he's scared of someone,' Jesse said.

'If you were in business with Moon Monaghan, who would you be scared of?' I said.

'Cronjager says Buddy's movie company is located in LA. He's got some forensic accounting people looking at it.'

'They usually make a corporation for a specific project,' I said. 'Tony Gault told me that.'

'Sounds like that's the case here,' Jesse said. 'This company is Warrior Productions.'

'I don't know what they will find out,' I said. 'But here's what I think happened.'

'I'm all ears,' Jesse said.

'Well,' I said. 'Not all.'

Jesse grinned.

'I may blush,' he said. 'What's your theory?'

'I think Moon invested a lot in Buddy and even though the pictures did well, Buddy doesn't show a profit.'

'Creative accounting,' Jesse said. 'Remember, I used to live there.'

'So Moon wants his money,' I said. 'He pressures Cousin Arlo, who pressures Buddy, but he can't pressure him all that hard, because Buddy lives three thousand miles away with a bunch of bodyguards in a big, inaccessible house. Close to Moon, actually. But Moon isn't working on Buddy, at least not yet. Arlo was the one who got him to invest. Arlo's supposed to get it back. Moon, however, doesn't care about bodyguards and miles. Moon wants his money.'

'And we know Moon's collection methods.'

'Exactly. He doesn't kill Buddy, because then Buddy won't ever be able to pay him. So he kills somebody else to scare Buddy.'

'And, knowing a little about Moon, to punish them for getting him into a sour deal.'

'Yes,' I said.

'So you say Moon killed the two guys in LA?'

'Yes.'

'And Misty?'

'I don't know,' I said. 'All that security? And it doesn't seem Moon's style, sneak somebody in and break her neck.'

'Maybe he bought off the security,' Jesse said. 'Let Buddy see that Moon could get in there, security or not.'

'Maybe.'

'Who else we got?'

'Gerard, Buddy, or Erin,' I said.

'That's my list, too,' Jesse said. 'We may get something from Cronjager in a few days.'

'Or a few weeks,' I said.

'Depends,' Jesse said. 'Cronjager likes to clear cases.'

Jesse looked at me for a moment without expression.

'Shall I lock the door?' he said.

'Fancy boutiques,' I said, 'okay. But I draw the line at squad rooms.'

He grinned.

55

It was nearly noon when I came calling. Buddy was in his atrium, having some waffles served by a maid in a little uniform. He wore a maroon polo shirt with white velour sweatpants and tan snakeskin loafers. His waist rolled out a little over the top of his sweatpants, and his arms were thin and soft-looking.

'Hey, Sunny Randall,' he said. 'Girl gumshoe, what do you know?'

'A lot and nothing,' I said. 'Can we chat while you eat?'

'Sure. I love company. Want something? Coffee? Juice? Want some waffles?'

'No,' I said. 'Thank you.'

Outside the atrium glass it was still snowing, though it still was falling as if it didn't mean it. The ocean looked unpleasant, slate-colored and choppy.

'So tell me what you know and what you don't,' Buddy said.

'First a question,' I said.

'Shoot' – Buddy snickered – 'in a manner of speaking.'

'Did your first *Woman Warrior* picture make money?'

'Sure did,' Buddy said. 'That franchise has been a damn cash cow, you know?'

'Did it show a profit?'

Buddy was spreading butter on his waffle. He paused with the knife in mid-spread and frowned a little.

'Why you want to know?'

'I'm a detective,' I said. 'I like to know things.'

'Well, Sunny Bunny,' he said, 'movie business ain't easy to explain. And that was a while ago. I don't remember the details now. But I can tell you that Buddy made out like fucking gangbusters, okay?'

'Sure, Buddy,' I said. 'Who financed the first one?'

Buddy put his knife down.

'Sunny,' he said, 'lemme make a couple of points here. I got a lotta enterprises going. Movies is just one of them. I can't be running the kind of thing that Buddy Bollen runs and worry about small specifics from five years back.'

'So you don't remember?'

'Correct,' Buddy said. 'And my second point: It's none of your fucking business.'

'Did Arlo help arrange financing?' I said.

'Arlo?'

'Arlo Delaney. He was partners with Greg Newton.'

'What the fuck are you doing?' Buddy asked.

'I'm investigating,' I said.

'Well don't investigate me, for crissake. I'm the one hired you.'

'Actually, Erin hired me,' I said.

'Yeah, and I'm paying you.'

'Your choice,' I said. 'Do you know Arlo Delaney?'

He was silent, looking at his waffles.

'How about Moon Monaghan?' I said.

Buddy sat back in his chair. He stayed like that for a time without further movement. Studying the indentations in his waffle.

'You think I know them, don't you?' he said.

'I believe I can prove it,' I said.

He sat some more.

'What can you prove?' he said.

'I believe I can prove that Gerard helped you get financing through Arlo Delaney, that it came from Moon Monaghan, and that to secure your continued support, Misty and Erin had to regularly have sex with you. Often together.'

'You could get in on that,' Buddy said, 'you want to.'

'I don't want to,' I said. 'You have any comment on what I can prove?'

'By prove,' Buddy said, 'I assume somebody told you this – so it would be my word against his, or hers.'

'There are several hims or hers,' I said. 'Plus, the LA police are doing some forensic accounting.'

'On me?' Buddy said.

'I don't know where they're starting, but it will get to you. And when they do, I suspect I'll be able to prove that you cooked the books on the first *Woman Warrior* and the investors got stiffed. And since I'm pretty sure that the principal investor was Moon Monaghan, you are then implicated in two murders in LA. It would also explain the security here.'

'That's for Erin.'

'The hell it is,' I said.

'It's for both of us. We're larger-than-life people,' Buddy said. 'We need to be protected from the public.'

'And from Moon Monaghan, whom you stiffed.'

Buddy stood up suddenly and walked to the end of the atrium and looked out at the sweep of his snow-dressed lawn. Then he turned and looked back down the atrium at me.

'Say it's true. I'm not saying it is, but if it was, you think I killed Misty?'

'No,' I said. 'Misty wasn't Erin, maybe, she was a big, strong, agile girl; you don't look to me like you could snap the neck on a canary.'

Buddy's face flushed.

'You think like a loser,' Buddy said. 'I can hire people for anything I need.'

'Did you?'

'To kill Misty?'

'Yes.'

'Why would I?' he said. 'I liked the sister thing. It was like they would compete with each other. See who could be hotter.'

Ick!

'We're going to prove all of this. It would just speed things up a little if you confirmed my theory,' I said. 'Also make all of us like you better when the time comes to reckon it all up.'

'Us?'

'Me and the police.'

'LA too?'

'Yes.'

'You're connected in LA?'

'Yes.'

Buddy walked slowly down to the breakfast table again. He picked up his waffle and took a bite out of it like it was a piece of toast. He chewed, swallowed, made a dissatisfied face, and threw the rest of the waffle back on the plate.

'Mostly you got it right,' he said. 'Except I don't know nothing about anybody getting killed in LA and I don't know about Misty getting killed.'

'But you did finance your movie with Moon Monaghan through his cousin Arlo?'

'Yeah.'

'And then you flimflammed him on the net profit?'

'Moon was hot to be a player,' Buddy said. 'But he didn't know the rules of the game, you know? … And I did.'

'You might have been wise,' I said, 'to find out Moon's rules, too.'

'Don't matter,' Buddy said. 'He can't get to me.'

Suddenly Buddy raised his head and looked straight at me.

'Nobody can,' he said.

'And you know Gerard,' I said.

'Basgall? Sure. He used to come around every once in a while, visit the girls.'

'He was here at the time Misty was killed.'

'Yeah? If you say so.'

We looked at each other. Having heard the worst, Buddy seemed to have recovered. In a little while he'd be calling me Sunny Bunny again.

'Do you have any ideas,' I said, 'on who killed Misty?'

He shook his head.

'Be your department, Samantha Spade,' he said.

56

I sat with Felix in a booth at a faux-Irish pub in Allston. We each had a draft beer in a pint glass. Rosie sat with us. I was pretty sure that dogs weren't allowed even in Irish bars in Allston. But she was sitting in Felix's lap, and no one seemed prepared to speak on the subject.

'I talked to Moon,' Felix said. 'About the bozo he sent to talk to you.'

'How does Moon feel about that?' I said. 'Spike was pretty, ah, direct.'

'I told Moon it was lucky the tough fag was there, because you'd have shot the bozo if the tough fag wasn't there.'

'Spike,' I said.

'Yeah, sure, Spike. Anyway, the bozo's just day labor. Moon don't care.'

'Good.'

'I told Moon that me and Desmond had a special interest in you, even though you wasn't married to Richie anymore.'

'Does Desmond really feel that way?' I said.

'No. You ain't married to his kid anymore, Desmond don't much give a shit anymore. But I do, and me and Desmond been brothers a long time.'

'And using both your names would impress Moon,' I said.

'Moon don't want trouble with the Burkes,' Felix said. 'He won't bother you no more.'

'How about the, ah, bozo?' I said. 'You think he'll make a return visit, even things out, perhaps?'

'Nope.'

I looked hard at Felix.

'You sound sure.'

'He won't be back,' Felix said.

'Felix?'

'Take my word.'

'Did you … ?'

'Don't ask,' Felix said, and made the growly sound he thought was a laugh. 'Don't tell.'

'Felix,' I said. 'I don't …'

'Anybody ask you?' he said.

'How did you even know about this?'

'The tough fag called me.'

'Spike,' I said.

'Yeah,' Felix said. 'Spike.'

'I appreciate you looking out for me, Felix,' I said. 'I appreciate Spike, too. But I can't have you killing people for me.'

'I kill who I kill,' Felix said. 'You got no say.'

I was quiet. I knew it was true. Felix sat there with Rosie in his lap, patting her gently with his enormous, thick hand. In his way he loved her. In his way he loved me. It was a scary way. But it was real. And the ugly truth of the matter was, I wouldn't miss the bozo.

'Do you know anyone Moon might use,' I said, 'who would snap a woman's neck with his hands?'

Felix drank some beer and patted his lips with a paper napkin.

'Ain't that hard to do,' Felix said. 'Moon would know plenty of guys could do it.'

'Is there anyone who would, what, specialize?' I said.

Felix smiled. I think.

'Nobody I know of, that specialized,' he said.

'Is it a good way to kill somebody?'

'They're all good,' Felix said. 'Depends what you want. Try to make it look like an accident? Maybe. Probably don't work. Most MEs can spot that pretty quick. Got to do it real quiet? Maybe, no gunshots, nothing like that. But if you miss it first try, you get a lot of screaming.'

'And you might miss it,' I said.

Felix made his growly sound again.

'Sure,' he said. 'You don't get to practice too much.'

'So if you were sneaking into a heavily guarded place to kill a woman, what would you use?'

'Knife,' Felix said. 'You're any good at all, you can cut her throat and even if she don't die right away, she don't make any noise.'

I nodded.

'You thinking about Moon for the murder you're working on, that broad in Paradise?'

'Yes.'

'Broad ever leave the house?' Felix said.

'Often.'

'Alone?'

'I suppose. I don't really know. But there should have been no reason not to,' I said. 'So why not do it then? Why do it in a heavily guarded compound?'

Felix nodded.

'Wasn't Moon,' he said.

57

'So you're saying Buddy's too puny to have broken her neck?' Jesse said.

'Yes. Not just because he is puny. But because he knows he's puny. He wouldn't try it.'

Jesse nodded.

'And Felix says that Moon wouldn't kill her that way?'

'He does.'

'Felix is probably right,' Jesse said. 'If he killed her as a warning to Buddy, it wouldn't be like that. Too much risk, not enough gain.'

'Moon's way would be the two guys in LA.'

'Which would make Moon Cronjager's problem,' Jesse said. 'If we're right.'

'You could put Cronjager in touch with Captain Healy,' I said.

'Already did.'

'He probably ought to talk with Martin Quirk, too,' I said. 'My father knows him.'

'The Boston homicide boss. Healy said he'd do that.'

'Way ahead of me,' I said.

'Remember,' he said, 'I am THE CHIEF!'

'I know,' I said. 'I have to fight this compulsion to salute.'

Jesse's eyes brightened for a moment.

'That's how I felt,' Jesse said, 'in Jere Jillian's dressing room.'

I felt as if I might be blushing.

'Will you please let that go?' I said.

'Absolutely not,' he said.

I shook my head.

'So, if I'm right about Buddy,' I said, 'and Felix is right about Moon, then we're down to Erin or Gerard.'

'Or a mysterious person or persons unknown,' Jesse said.

'How useful a theory is that?'

'Useless,' Jesse said. 'Unless Erin and Gerard turn out not to have done it.'

'So let's assume one of them did,' I said.

'Or both,' Jesse said.

'Or both.'

We sat for a moment in Jesse's office and contemplated the state of our theory.

'A motive would be nice,' I said.

'Why would Erin kill her sister?' Jesse said.

'By breaking her neck,' I said. 'I would think that would be sort of a rage thing. I mean, it takes someone pretty cold to walk into the exercise room planning to snap her sister's neck.'

'Might have been an accident.'

'They had a fight and Misty's neck got broken?'

'Could happen,' Jesse said.

'The medical examiner says someone was holding her face.'

Jesse got up and came around the desk.

'Here,' he said. 'Stand up and take hold of my face.'

I did.

'Now,' he said, 'suppose we're having a vigorous discussion about ... oh, say, the dressing room at Jere Jillian.'

'Stop it,' I said.

'And you're holding my face to keep my attention, and I'm twisting to get away, maybe, if you're strong, and I twist one way and you twist the other ...'

'I see what you mean,' I said. 'I don't think it could happen with you and me. But Erin's stronger than I am, and maybe Misty's neck isn't as strong as yours.'

Jesse sat back down at his desk.

'And of course,' Jesse said, 'Gerard's strong enough.'

'The only people who know if our theory of the case is correct,' I said, 'would be Erin and Gerard.'

'And if they keep shut up we're screwed,' Jesse said. 'We got nowhere to go.'

'I can keep talking to Erin,' I said. 'She's a pretty messy emotional scene.'

'Got little choice,' Jesse said. 'Gerard's three thousand miles away, and not likely to do anything stupid.'

'If he thought Erin were in jeopardy,' I said.

'Because he loves her?'

I nodded.

'You still believe him, that he loves Erin?' Jesse said.

'I do,' I said. 'He might kill her for Erin.'

'I'm taking your word on this one,' Jesse said.

'Because I'm a woman?'

Jesse grinned again. 'Because of the dressing room,' he said.

'That wasn't about love,' I said.

'No?'

'No. That was about fun.'

'Just fun?'

'Yes,' I said. 'Of course, I wouldn't have done that with someone I didn't like. But it wasn't lovemaking. It was play.'

Jesse tilted back in his chair and stared at me. 'Is that good or bad?'

I thought about Richie, and about other men, and about Dr Silverman. I thought about Jesse.

'When I was with Richie,' I said, 'we were always careful to call it lovemaking. Never sex. Never cute names like "poon tang." Never ever called it "fucking." We always thought that was sort of dehumanizing.'

Jesse was quiet. He seemed to be listening with all of himself. It was one of the things that made him different from most people. Probably made him a good cop. He listened completely.

'But if it was lovemaking,' I said, 'what happened if one of us didn't want to, for instance? Did it mean we didn't love one another?'

'Shouldn't,' Jesse said.

'But it did. The act of sex came with too much weight attached.'

'God yes,' Jesse said.

'You understand,' I said.

'I did the same thing,' he said. 'Everything Jenn and I did sexually was she loves me, she loves me not.'

'When you love someone,' I said, 'everything you do is making love. Having breakfast, food shopping ...'

'Talking about a murder case,' Jesse said.

'Talking about a murder case,' I said.

We had come awfully close to it and we both knew we had. We were silent for a minute.

'So in that sense,' Jesse said after a while, 'sex is making love. Like breakfast.'

'Yes. And if it doesn't work one day, it's no worse than burning the toast.'

'Maybe you and I both required more of sex than sex can deliver,' Jesse said.

'It might be fine if it was just sex. Fun in the context of love.'

'Wow,' Jesse said. 'You've been talking to your shrink.'

I nodded.

'Maybe I'll talk to mine,' he said.

58

At the time I thought of it as better to be lucky than good. In retrospect maybe it was because Jesse and I kept pushing and poking until we finally dislodged something. Whatever it was, it resulted in Erin calling me at ten minutes before noon on Tuesday morning.

'You have to help me,' she said.

'Okay.'

'I'm on my cell phone ... in the bathroom ... with the door locked ... so they can't hear me.'

'They?'

'Buddy,' she said. 'He won't let me leave. He says I'm hysterical. He says I'm crazy.'

'What do you want me to do?' I said.

'Come get me.'

'Will he let me take you?' I said.

'No. But you can do something. I have to get out of here.'

'Are you in danger?'

'I have to get out,' she said.

I could hear the tremor in her voice. Buddy may have been right. She sounded hysterical.

'I have to get out,' she said. 'I have to go someplace... You have to take me ... security ... everywhere. I have to get out.'

'I'll come right over,' I said.

'They won't let you in.'

'I'll think of something,' I said.

I called Jesse from the car.

'Something's up with Erin Flint,' I said.
'Good,' he said. 'Tell me.'
I told him.
'Okay,' Jesse said. 'I'll meet you there. We don't want to make a federal case out of this. We'll tell them I wish to bring her in for questioning. Which will be true.'
We hung up. We went through the Ted Williams Tunnel, past the airport and Orient Heights. As we passed Suffolk Downs, Rosie, who had been asleep on the passenger seat beside me, stood up suddenly and jumped onto the floor. She curled up close to the heater vent, put one paw on top of her nose, and went back to sleep. After we figured Erin Flint out, maybe we could think about Rosie for a while.
Jesse was there in front of SeaChase when I arrived, sitting in a squad car with the big, young cop I'd seen before. Named after some ballplayer I'd forgotten.
'You and Rosie hop in,' Jesse said. 'We'll run the gate gauntlet together.'
We got in the back. Rosie looked annoyed at being removed from her heater, but then she saw Jesse and gave a big wag, and all was forgiven.
'Take her in, Suit,' Jesse said.
Suitcase Simpson.
'Take her in?' Suit said.
'I been watching some old navy war movies,' Jesse said.
The cruiser pulled up to the gate. Jesse smiled at the gate guard and held up his badge.
'I'll have to call ahead, sir,' the guard said.
'Obviously,' Jesse said pleasantly, 'you don't realize that I'm the fucking chief of fucking police. For the fucking chief of fucking police you open now, and call after.'
'I …'
'Open it.'
The guard opened the gate and we headed up the long driveway. There were the usual blazers around, and Randy, the head blazer, met us at the door. We got out.
'You and Rosie hold her steady here,' Jesse said to Suit.
'Jesus,' Suit said, 'I hope you don't start watching musicals.'

Jesse grinned. He was wearing jeans and a blue softball jacket. His badge was clipped to the jacket near the neck.

'We need to see Miss Flint,' Jesse said to Randy.

'Miss Flint is indisposed,' Randy said.

'Dispose her,' Jesse said.

Randy's face was expressionless.

'Wait here, please,' he said, and turned down the hall. Jesse nodded at me and we went right behind him.

'Excuse me,' Randy said. 'Don't you need a warrant?'

'I have reason to believe that Miss Flint is being held against her will. I need no warrant.'

'Against her will?'

'Get her out here, Randy.'

'Buddy said …'

'That's right, *Buddy said.* So she *is* being held against her will.'

'Wait a minute,' Randy said.

'Sunny,' Jesse said to me. 'Is "held against her will" sort of like kidnapping?'

'I believe so,' I said. 'And kidnapping is, like, a really big felony.'

'To which you, Randy, appear to be an accessory.'

Randy was silent for a moment. We stood in the vast hallway and waited.

'Okay,' he said. 'I'll get her.'

'And we'll go with you,' I said.

Randy looked at Jesse. Jesse did an 'after you' gesture, and the three of us headed down the hall. Erin's bedroom was in the medieval castle wing of SeaChase. The door was wide oak planking with black iron strap hinges. Randy knocked.

'Miss Flint,' he said. 'The police are here.'

I said, 'Erin it's me, Sunny.'

The door opened. Erin stared at Jesse and looked at me.

'Chief Stone and I need you to come down to police headquarters,' I said.

'Now, please, Miss Flint,' Jesse said.

Erin put on a long, silver coat, made of suede, with a fur collar, and followed us out. In the downstairs hallway Buddy was standing, with a can of Coke in his hand.

'What the hell is going on?' he said.

'Step aside,' Jesse said.

'Where the fuck are you going with her?'

We kept walking. Buddy's voice went up an octave.

'You fucking hick,' Buddy said. 'You wanna keep your fucking job you'll hold it right there.'

We kept walking toward the front door.

'I said hold it,' Buddy shrieked and stepped in front of us.

'Buddy,' Jesse said. 'If you interfere with a police officer in the performance of his duty I will have to arrest you, and in the process, you may lose some teeth.'

'You threatening me?' Buddy said.

Jesse nodded.

'You keep your mouth shut, Erin,' he trilled. 'I'll be down there with my lawyer.'

Jesse looked at me.

'Oh, oh,' he said. 'The lawyers.'

'I'm all atremble.'

I took Erin's hand and we walked out of the house. Jesse followed behind. From the open doorway Buddy was screaming at me.

'And I'll get you fucking disbarred, bitch.'

Erin and I got in the back. I still had her hand. She was shaking. Rosie, who had been up in front with Suit, jumped in back with me. Erin shrank a little away from her but was quiet. Jesse got in the front. He turned and grinned at us.

'I didn't know Buddy knew your nickname,' Jesse said to me.

'He got the threat wrong, too,' I said.

Jesse nodded. 'Take her home, Suit,' he said.

Suit shook his head slowly as he put the cruiser in gear.

'Jesus Christ,' he said.

59

As we rolled across the causeway, Erin said, 'I didn't want the police.'

'I know,' I said. 'But there was no other way. They had me outnumbered.'

Jesse turned sideways in the front seat to talk with us.

'Where would you like to go?' Jesse said.

'Go?'

'Yes,' Jesse said. 'You're out of there, where would you like to go?'

'You said you were taking me to the police station.'

'I made that up,' Jesse said.

'We used that to get you out of there,' I said. 'Now, if you'll tell us what you need and where you want to go and why, maybe we can help you.'

'I …'

Rosie wiggled down between us and got herself comfortable. Erin looked down at her.

'Why do you take this dog everywhere?' Erin said.

'I love her,' I said. 'Tell us what you need.'

Erin tried to think of what she should do. We waited.

As we reached the other side of the causeway, Erin said, 'I have to see Gerard.'

'Where is he?' I said.

'Here,' Erin said.

'Here where?' I said.

'Here, Boston, in a hotel.'

Suit looked at Jesse; Jesse nodded. Suit headed straight out past the beach at the end of the causeway, not right to downtown and police headquarters.

'What is he doing here?' I said.

'I called him,' Erin said. 'I have to see him.'

'Why?'

Erin's breath came heavily, as if she'd just finished a sprint. She didn't speak. I didn't press her. We rode in silence for a while. Erin's breathing didn't improve.

Finally she said, 'My life is falling apart. I'm falling apart… My sister's dead… If I play baseball, I'll be a laughing stock… Buddy says if I don't play, I won't make any more movies… He says I'm already a laughing stock as an actress… I have to do ugly sex things with him… I need Gerard. I have to see Gerard.'

'Because?' I said.

'Because he loves me. He's the only one. He loves me. I have to see him.'

I looked at Jesse. He raised his eyebrows, but he nodded.

'Okay, we'll take you to him. Where is he?'

'He won't like there being anybody else.'

'It's the only way you'll get to him,' I said.

There were tears on Erin's face. I took her hand again. Our held hands rested on Rosie's back. If Rosie minded, she didn't say so.

'Make a deal with us,' I said.

'I got nobody else,' she said. 'Just Gerard.'

'And us,' I said.

She turned her head away from me and stared out the window of the car at the expensive houses we were passing.

'Gerard came all this way,' I said, 'because you called him?'

Erin nodded.

'We came and got you out of Buddy's house,' I said, 'because you called me.'

She nodded again.

'Jesse and I will go in with you. The four of us will sit down, you and Gerard, me and Jesse. We will talk this out. We will find a way to help you.'

'Stop the car,' Erin said. 'I want to call him and I don't want you to hear me.'

Suit looked at Jesse. Jesse nodded. Suit pulled the car over. Erin got out with her cell phone and walked twenty feet away.

'What if she runs?' I said.

'Suit is like a gazelle,' Jesse said.

'When did that happen?' Suit said.

'Maybe it's me that's like a gazelle,' Jesse said.

Erin spoke for a while on her cell phone. Then she folded up her cell phone and walked back to the car.

'He's at the Four Seasons,' Erin said. 'He gave me the room number.'

'And he'll wait?' I said.

'Gerard loves me,' she said.

Her breathing was better.

'So he'll wait.'

'Yes.'

'Do you love him?' I said.

'Love him?'

'Yes.'

'I ... I ... don't even know what that means,' Erin said. 'But I have to see him.'

I nodded.

'My guess would be, *yes*,' I said.

60

We sat in the living room of Gerard's small suite, with a view of the Public Garden, and across Charles Street, the Common. Erin sat beside Gerard on a couch.

'I wanna thank you for getting her out,' Gerard said.

I nodded. Jesse nodded.

'Why didn't he want you out?' I said.

Erin looked at Gerard. Gerard nodded.

'He was afraid I'd tell people I wasn't good at baseball,' Erin said. 'And I said I would if I wanted. And maybe I'd tell people what a sick pig he was in bed.'

'Why did he want you so badly to play?' I said.

'Because he said the team was losing money, and if he could bring in a bunch of people to see me play, then he could pump up the price and sell it.'

Gerard was quiet. He looked at Jesse, and Jesse looked back at him. There seemed to be some sort of male appraisal thing going on.

'Why did he want to sell it?' I said.

'He said it was my fault, that he had to get some money to pay off a guy who had lost a fortune backing my *Woman Warrior* movies.'

'Moon Monaghan,' I said.

She looked at Gerard. Gerard nodded.

'Yes,' she said.

'You didn't lose him money,' Gerard said.

'Buddy says so.'

Gerard didn't answer.

'And what happened to Misty?' I said.

Jesse and Gerard looked at each other some more. Erin was silent.

'Come on, Erin,' I said. 'We've come this far. We can't help you if we don't know the score.'

She shook her head. I waited. Gerard was rubbing his chin with the back of his hand, still looking at Jesse.

'I killed her,' he said.

'No,' Erin said. 'No, he didn't.'

And then I knew. I didn't know why yet. But I knew.

'You killed her?' I said.

'Yes.'

'Erin,' Gerard said. 'Shut up. She's just trying to protect me.'

'Or vice versa,' I said. 'How did it happen, Erin?'

'She was going to leave. She told me that she was sick of doing it with Buddy, all the sick shit he liked. And she wasn't a movie star and she wasn't going to be a baseball star and she was going to leave me. We been together all our lives. Buddy said, she left, he'd throw me out, too. He didn't need either one of us.'

She paused.

'That's all true,' Gerard said flatly. 'Except I killed her. Erin called me. She always called me when it got bad. And I came out to talk with Misty. And I grabbed her by the face, trying to reason with her ...'

He put his hands up to show how he'd put them on each side of Misty's face.

'And she tried to twist away and I twisted back and ...' He shrugged.

'Her neck snapped,' I said.

Gerard nodded.

'It was an accident. I didn't want to hurt her. I loved her like a sister,' Gerard said.

'That's right,' Erin said. 'That's what happened, but it was me. I'm a very strong woman. Stronger than Misty. Gerard tried to talk sense to her but she was crazy mad and like he said, I put my hands on her face ... I did it. I didn't mean to, but I did it.'

Gerard shook his head.

'It was me,' he said.

'And Buddy knew this?' I said to Erin.

'Yes. He said I did anything crazy he'd turn me in.'

'So what did you want Gerard to do?'

'After I killed Misty?'

'Now,' I said.

'I wanted him … I wanted him to kill Buddy and take me away.'

'Too much security,' Jesse said.

'Yep,' Gerard said. 'But once she was out of there, I was willing to wait.'

'Why bother?' I said. 'Once he's sure Buddy won't pay up, Moon will do it for you.'

Gerard nodded and almost smiled.

'Probably,' he said.

'So,' Jesse said. 'You both agree that Misty's death was accidental?'

They nodded.

'But you don't agree who did it?'

'I did,' Gerard said.

'I did it,' Erin said.

Jesse looked at me.

'That,' Jesse said to them, still looking at me, 'could present a very interesting legal dilemma for someone trying to prosecute the case.'

Nobody said anything.

'If you want to go to trial with it,' Jesse said, 'I can put you in touch with the best criminal defense lawyer in the state.'

Jesse's gaze was steady on me.

'And if we don't want to go to trial?' Gerard said.

Jesse kept looking at me.

'If you deny this conversation and insist you don't know anything about Misty's death,' Jesse said, 'I'm not sure I got a case.'

'You could work on Buddy,' Gerard said carefully.

'I could,' Jesse said.

'Or,' I said, 'Chief Stone and I could admit defeat.'

'Which means what?' Gerard said, even more carefully.

Jesse stood suddenly.

'You and Erin go back to California,' he said. 'And don't come to Paradise anymore.'

I stood and we walked to the door. Erin and Gerard were staring at us. At the door Jesse paused.

'Don't push it too hard,' he said. 'You kill Buddy and I'll nail you for it.'

Erin said, 'Sunny ...'
Jesse opened the door.
'*Vaya con Dios*,' I said.
And we left.

61

Jesse and I were in South Boston in my loft, drinking martinis. I had just given Rosie a carrot, one of her favorites, and she was making a lot of noise crunching it up.

'I knew I was soft,' I said. 'I didn't realize you were, too.'

'The woman has been somebody's product all her life. She's been having sex with Buddy Bollen for years now.'

'Ugh,' I said.

'I believe her story about her sister,' he said. 'And I believe she did it.'

'But Gerard saying he did it bought him a lot.'

'Some,' Jesse said. 'Though he too might have noticed the usefulness of the defense.'

'Still, he came when she called,' I said. 'Both times.'

Jesse nodded.

'He loves her,' I said. 'She loves him.'

'Or something,' Jesse said. 'Those are two fucked-up people.'

'And they needed a break,' I said.

'Yeah.'

'So you gave them one.'

'We gave them one,' Jesse said. 'I'm not taking the rap alone.'

'I don't have to stand up in public and say I can't solve the case.'

'I don't, either,' Jesse said. 'We'll just keep it open, and in time something else will get people's attention.'

'Like the murder of Buddy Bollen,' I said.

'That won't happen until Moon has exhausted everything else,' Jesse said.

'And we're just going to let Buddy slide? He must have done something wrong.'

'Let's see what Cronjager's forensic accountants come up with,' Jesse said. 'One way or another, there's no good news for Buddy in the days ahead.'

I got up and went to the stove where I was making beef bourguignon, one of the three things I could cook. I checked it, lowered the heat a little, made another shaker of martinis, and gave Rosie another carrot. I brought the shaker back to the table and freshened our drinks.

'You are every bit as sentimental as I am.'

'A fool for love,' Jesse said.

'Like me,' I said.

We looked at each other.

'It'll be an hour or so before dinner is ready,' I said.

'Shall we go out and find an exclusive dress shop?' Jesse said.

'Let's try for more conventional fun tonight,' I said. 'My bed is right there.'

'And what it lacks in exotic,' Jesse said, 'it makes up in handy.'

'I think maybe I love you,' I said.

It surprised me. I hadn't intended to say it. In fact I didn't quite know until now that I felt it.

'Yes,' Jesse said. 'I think I might love you, too.'

'Isn't that amazing?' I said.

'Yes,' Jesse said. 'It is.'

We touched glasses and took a drink and put the glasses down.

'Have you shaved your legs?' Jesse said.

'Every day,' I said, 'since I met you.'

Robert B. Parker's *WONDERLAND*

Written by Ace Atkins

Henry Cimoli and Spenser have been friends for years, yet the old boxing trainer has never asked the private eye for a favor. Until now. A heavy-handed developer is trying to buy up Henry's condo on Revere Beach and sends thugs to move the process along. Soon Spenser and his apprentice, Zebulon Sixkill, find a trail leading to a mysterious and beautiful woman, a megalomaniacal Las Vegas kingpin, and plans to turn a chunk of land north of Boston into a sprawling casino. Bitter rivals emerge, alliances turn, and the uglier pieces of the Boston political machine look to put an end to Spenser's investigation.

Aspiration, greed, and twisted dreams all focus on the old Wonderland dog track where the famous amusement park once fronted the ocean. For Spenser and Z, this simple favor to Henry will become the fight of their lives.

noexit.co.uk

978-1-84344-281-3

Ebook available.

192pp

£7.99

Robert B. Parker in Ebook

The following backlist titles are available from No Exit Press

noexit.co.uk

The Spenser Novels

9781843441618	Small Vices
9781843442974	Sudden Mischief
9781842439937	Hush Money
9781843441656	Hugger Mugger
9781843442301	Potshot
9781843442387	Widow's Walk
9781843441694	Back Story
9781843441731	Bad Business
9781843442349	Cold Service
9781843443001	School Days
9781843443032	Dream Girl
9781843442424	Now & Then
9781843442820	Wonderland
9781843443483	Silent Night

The Jesse Stone Mysteries

9781842439968	Night Passage
9781842439999	Trouble in Paradise
9781843442226	Death in Paradise
9781843442189	Stone Cold
9781843443063	Sea Change
9781843443278	High Profile
9781843443520	Damned If I Do

The Sunny Randall Mysteries

9781843443124	Family Honor
9781842434932	Perish Twice
9781843443155	Shrink Rap
9781843443186	Melancholy Baby
9781843443216	Blue Screen
9781843443094	Spare Change

Also by Robert B Parker

9781843443247	Double Play

Robert B. Parker (1932–2010) has long been acknowledged as the dean of American crime fiction. His novels featuring the wise-cracking, street-smart Boston private eye Spenser earned him a devoted following and reams of critical acclaim, typified by RWB Lewis' comment, 'We are witnessing one of the great series in the history of the American detective story' (*The New York Times Book Review*).

Born and raised in Massachusetts, Parker attended Colby College in Maine, served with the Army in Korea, and then completed a PhD in English at Boston University. He married his wife Joan in 1956; they raised two sons, David and Daniel. Together the Parkers founded Pearl Productions, a Boston-based independent film company named after their short-haired pointer, Pearl, who has also been featured in many of Parker's novels.

Robert B. Parker died in 2010 at the age of 77.